# Patricia Backhaus

To Dorillee—
Best wishes to my
Choral buddy.
6/8/18

## The Last Rose of Summer

### A Concert Band Mystery with Recipes

# Table of Contents

The mystery you are about to read is a product of my imagination. Some of the characters in this entertainment were real people, but none of them, to the best of my knowledge, was ever involved in a police investigation. They are historical figures to help set the time period, and to whet your curiosity about band music history. Enjoy!

## The Players

* Real musician
+ Real person
♫ Real band

### Smith Family

Richard Cottingham Smith
Elisabeth Woolforth Smith
Richard Danforth Smith
*Vashti Anne Smith, French horn
Reginald Woolforth Smith
Hettie McGrew, domestic

### O'Toole Family

Daniel O'Toole, Master Woodwind Craftsman & clarinet
Mary O'Toole, deceased

### O'Brien Family

Sgt. Sean Patrick O'Brien, cornet
Molly O'Brien
Jack O'Brien, ophicleide
Erin O'Brien
Rachel O'Brien
George O'Brien
Ian O'Brien
Mary O'Brien

### Blackthorne Family

Otis Simpson Blackthorne, cornet
Sara Breen Blackthorne

Alice Marie Blackthorne, cornet
Margaret Mary Blackthorne, cornet

## Betsy Ross All-Lady Silver Cornet Band

Margaret Mary Blackthorne, Directress
+Amanda Fetkenheuer, solo cornet
Christina Swenson, piccolo
Sadie Thomas, tuba
Cybil Hayes, snare drum
Lily Beauchamp, euphonium

## C.G. Conn

Arthur Ritberger, Proprietor, flautist
Daniel O'Toole, Master Woodwind Craftsman, clarinetist
Bruno Stein, Master Brass Craftsman, double bell euphonium
Jack O'Brien, Apprentice, ophicleide
Mrs. Tudor, helper

## Pick-Penn Smelting & Iron Works

Henry Casswell, bandsman
Mr. Kitridge, plant supervisor
Mr. Young, assistant

## Blackthorne Bunting Works

Mr. Robert Hintz, plant supervisor
Stanley Robinson, driver
Mrs. Sawyer, floor manager

## Local Constabulary

Sean Patrick O'Brien, Police Sergeant, cornet
William "Flash" Manily, photographer
Dr. Mortimer "Morty" Harrison, coroner
Adam Brinkman, patrolman, alto horn
Tom Ralfus, patrolman, rudimental drummer
Chief Miller
Evans, dispatcher

## Supporting Players

William Casswell, billiard player
Major Howard Francis Darby
Phineas Forbes, caretaker of Philadelphia Founder's Hall
Mr. Higgins, President of the Benjamin Franklin Free Thinkers Society
The Hintzes, friends
Seamus O'Flaherty, shoe polisher
Rodney Starkie, billiard player
Bob Matthis, billiard player
Sven Torgalson, billiard player
Howard Ritche, billiard player
Randy Brewer, billiard player
Mr. Treeder, banker
Rosalie, the Swenson's domestic
Mr. Rassmusen, druggist
Mr. Leutzinger, shop keeper
Margaret Weatherbee, milliner
Bishop Beecher, Episcopalian minister
Mrs. Beecher
Mr. Leonard Yingling, florest
Mr. Thomas Ryan, attorney
Mrs. Landsmeyer, boarding house proprietress

## Bands

Betsy Ross All-Lady Silver Cornet Band
♫Brushton Colliary Band
Kendelton Boy's Band
Pick-Penn Company Band
Sons of Killarney Band
St. Bilfred Brass Band
♫Thomas P. Brooke's Chicago Marine Band

## Musical Selections

These compositions are all real. They were composed for concert band in this time period. The composers are all real as well.

| | |
|---|---|
| Brooke, T. P. | The Cycle Queen March |
| Cole, W.L. | Cupid's Arrow Waltz |
| Gilmore, Patrick S. | Dinner Bell Polka |
| Harris, Chas. K | Hearts |
| Hartmann, John | Home, Sweet Home – Air Varie cornet solo |
| Liberati, A. | Philadelphia Patriots March |
| Pryor, Arthur | Thoughts of Love, trombone solo |
| Rogers, Walter B. | The Volunteer, cornet solo |
| Root, Geo. F | The Vacant Chair |
| Rollinson, T.H. | Rocked in the Cradle of the Deep – Grand |
| Fantasia cornet solo | |
| Sousa, John Philip | The Liberty Bell March |
| | The Stars & Stripes Forever March |
| | Washington Post March |
| Southwell, George | Cake Walk Schottische |
| | Rough Riders March |
| | Victory Overture |
| Traditional ballad | The Last Rose of Summer |
| Verdi, Giuseppe | The Anvil Chorus from "Il Trovatore" |

♫

# Chapter 1

For three years now the ladies had attended their weekly Tuesday evening rehearsals of the Betsy Ross All-Lady Silver Cornet Band. Miss Margaret Blackthorne had started each of these young ladies on their band instruments. They were all in their mid-teens and early twenties. Tuesday evenings were very special as it gave each young musician an opportunity to be out and about and to dress up in her latest fashionable outfit.

Proper etiquette required that young ladies travel in pairs to avoid the appearance of impropriety. It helped to have the married ladies of the band as chaperones to the group when the band performed. For rehearsals the ladies would travel to Philadelphia's Founders Hall escorted by her father, mother (who often stayed in another part of the building visiting with other friends) or older brother. On this day Vashti Smith's older brother Richard Danforth Smith was her escort. Known to all as Danforth, he was tall and handsome in his Brooks Brother's suit. The other young ladies were glad to see him when he escorted Vashti into the hall.

"Hellooo, Danforth!" cooed Lily Beauchamp as she waved to him with her white lace hankie in her gloved hand. "How's MY Danny this evening." She giggled her way between him and his sister.

"Hello, Lily," said Vashti. "Perhaps you have forgotten that Danforth prefers to be called by his given name."

"Oh, Vashti, how can a sister know what her brother thinks in regard to his young lady?" She batted her eyelashes and phloophed her hankie.

"Thank you, Danforth. I'll see you later after rehearsal." Vashti gave her brother a quick exit so he could avoid Lily.

Vashti and Danforth had ridden to the rehearsal aboard the Philadelphia Rapid Transit (PRT, known as the Par- T) streetcar. These wonderful modern conveyances took passengers all around the city of Philadelphia for just a few cents.

"Hello, Vashti!" She turned to see Sadie Thomas entering the back stage area. Sadie and Vashti were best friends.

"Sadie! How wonderful it is to see you!"

"Let me guess. Lily was prowling the backstage area when you and Danforth came in tonight."

"Sadie, I'm going to have to come in the stage door by myself. That euphonium siren must get here at noon to be the first person we see coming in."

"I'm glad Danforth still brings you to rehearsal. I saw him outside just before I came in."

Vashti wondered if Sadie might be a little sweet on her brother. She would have to ask that another time. Right now she needed to prepare for rehearsal.

Cornet players were busy oiling their cornet valves. Reeds for the woodwinds were carefully placed on the rails of the mouthpieces and fastened on with a ligature. Drums were set up and the bass drum was tuned. Trombone slides were slicked up and tested, adding to the din of the cheerful voices.

The Betsy Ross All-Lady Silver Cornet Band was made up of a full compliment of band instruments. Though it was called a silver cornet band, it had all of the woodwinds, the middle and low brasses and battery. The battery was made up of snare drum, bass drum and cymbals. The "silver" in their name was a nod to the expensive, silver plated cornets that the cornet section played.

Three years before, a small group of ladies had ridden the PRT out to Willow Grove Park. Vashti, Sadie, Cybil Hayes, Amanda Fetkenheuer and Christina Swenson were there to hear the Thomas

P. Brooke's Chicago Marine Band. Once in the park the concerts were free, but one could pay an extra ten cents to sit under the pavilion by the bandstand. The friends had decided to stand.

It was not unusual to have thousands of people attending these wonderful events and standing up to listen. T.P. Brooke's Chicago Marine Band was a crackerjack group. After listening to them play Brooke's own *The Cycle Queen* march, the ensemble was determined to learn band instruments so that they could play in a band, too. Enter Miss Margaret Blackthorne, who became their directress and mentor. She was walking around the park and took notice of the ladies.

"Are you enjoying the band concert?" she inquired.

"Yes, very much," chimed in the friends in perfect unison.

"Perhaps you would be interested in joining a ladies band."

The lady with the soft British accent detailed for them her dream of creating a band for ladies. Now, nearly three years later and still musically inspired, the Betsy Ross All-Lady Silver Cornet Band was, once again, gathering to rehearse.

Philadelphia's Founder's Hall was a grandiose monument to civic pride. It was built of dazzlingly white Bedford limestone. The Great Hall was an auditorium that could seat eight thousand people. It had hosted concerts, political rallies, horticultural fairs and the annual October Reformation Festival Service held by the local Lutheran churches.

The stage area was built of elaborately decorative hardwoods forming a stunning *fleur de lis* at the front of the stage. This made it handsome space and advantageous to their practices as the acoustics enabled the musicians to tune and to balance their parts. Miss Blackthorne had pronounced it the perfect place to rehearse a band.

The ladies were all seated primly on stage of Philadelphia's Founders Hall. Band rehearsal had just begun. Most of the girls in the band had learned to play their instruments under the able tutelage of Miss Blackthorne. She smiled at them and stepped onto the podium.

"Remember to sit up straight, ladies. Posture is just as important in band as it is to proper etiquette and deportment for young ladies," reminded Miss Blackthorne.

Vashti Smith sat proudly forward on her chair holding her French horn as delicately as one could possibly do with an instrument that weighs thirty pounds. Vashti loved band music! Being a bit of a tomboy always set her apart from those girls who sat properly and spoke in soft, demure voices. She relished being active. As a little girl she was always running and climbing trees and loathed having bows in her hair. Though her mother had taught her to sew and embroider, to plan meals and to supervise a domestic staff, it suited her personality to be more rambunctious.

"Ladies, we will start with the unison playing of our concert B-flat scale. Those of you who are playing the drums should use the rhythm patterns that I wrote out for you. Horns up! One, two, three, breath."

Vashti passionately played her beautiful French horn, her somewhat unruly curls bouncing along to the beat.

When Vashti met Miss Blackthorne at Willow Grove Park, she returned home and begged her parents to allow her to learn a band instrument.

Her parents, Elisabeth Woolford and Richard Cottingham Smith had met at a lecture given by Ralph Waldo Emerson. Their love of literature and music drew them together and they were married the year after they met. Richard became a Professor of English literature at Heightsmore College in Philadelphia and they moved to the City of Brotherly Love to start their life together. Professor Smith was devoted to the works of many of the New England writers as he had met a good number of them. He was especially fond of the works of Edgar Allen Poe.

Elisabeth was an accomplished writer in her own right and was an occasional contributor of poems to the literary journal *The Dial*, published by Elizabeth Palmer Peabody. After marrying Richard and moving to Philadelphia, Elisabeth focused her attention toward running a household befitting an educated man. Her domicile was well run and she was adept at entertaining a wide variety of interesting faculty members from Heightsmore College as well as traveling literary people and musicians.

Her children, Richard Danforth, Vashti Anne and Reginald Woolford Smith arrived in even two-year intervals. All of the children, including Vashti, received a broad and progressive education.

"Now, ladies, let us start our rehearsal with John Philip Sousa's *The Stars & Stripes Forever March*", intoned Miss Blackthorne. "Check your key signatures and let's strive to keep the tempo lively."

When Vashti came to her parents for permission to learn a band instrument, they did not think it to be an unladylike pursuit, as many parents did. They thought it would be an excellent opportunity for her to expand her musical knowledge.

Professor Smith was excited about the instrument that she would play. "Have you chosen your instrument yet? What sounds do you like the best? Flute? Trombone? Drums? What interests you?" he asked, whirling his pipe in the air for added dramatic emphasis.

"Father," said Vashti, "I love the sound of the French horn. It's also pretty to look at with all those elegant twists and turns."

So Vashti took up the French horn, practiced her little heart out, and became passionately devoted to the impeccable playing of precise afterbeats in the music of John Philip Sousa and any other composer who deemed it appropriate for her to perform perfect "pahs". Vashti had been taught that each and every one of those notes was actually a solo for the horn section.

Miss Blackthorne stopped the band. "Ladies, ladies, ladies, how can we possibly play for the Ladies Auxiliary to the Benjamin Franklin

Free Thinker's Society's cakewalk if our rhythm is askew? I really must have precise downbeats and upbeats from the tubas, horns and back row cornets. Let me hear those musicians at the first strain."

The Ladies Auxiliary to the Benjamin Franklin Free Thinker's Society's cakewalk was an annual charitable event held to create scholarship money for a young person to attend a local college or preparatory school. Miss Blackthorne knew that this was a major social event of the season and she wanted the band to sound their best.

Sadie Thomas played tuba in the band. Sadie was tall and thin, not quite having filled out her form yet. She was tall enough to hold the tuba, so that was the instrument she played. Her pride and joy was a C.G. Conn Wonder model tuba with an upright bell that belonged to her uncle, who perished in the charge up San Juan Hill with Teddy Roosevelt's Rough Riders. She gets dewy-eyed every time the band plays George Southwell's *Rough Riders March*. In fact, Sadie has memorized the tuba part since she often cannot read the music through her tears.

Sadie grew up in a musical family and has taken to the tuba like a duck takes to water. Sadie and Vashti would get together to practice. Sadie played strong downbeats while Vashti inserted impeccable afterbeats. Soon the girls invited other friends to join in their practice sessions. Add in snare drummer Cybil Hayes, piccoloist Christina Swenson and solo cornetist Amanda Fetkenheuer, and it was a riot of sound for the neighbors with Sadie's "ooms" and Vashti's "pahs" leading the way.

"That's much better, ladies. When we play for the Ladies Auxiliary the pulse must be precise!"

Margaret Mary Blackthorne was the youngest daughter of Otis Simpson Blackthorne and Sara Breen Blackthorne. The family, including her older sister, Alice Marie Blackthorne, had emigrated from Great Britain shortly after the American Civil War. Otis Blackthorne was an accomplished cornet soloist with the Brushton Colliery Band by night and a clerk at the colliery store during the day. The Blackthornes had come to America seeking a better life. Mr. Blackthorne gained employment at the Pick-Penn Iron & Smelting Works as a smelter. It was hot, dirty work, but he was thrilled to be in the United States and to be able to provide for his family.

Pick-Penn also sponsored a company band. They had advertised in *The Bandmaster* magazine for a smelter who played the cornet. Otis was an outstanding cornetist, so they taught him how to smelt.

Alice and Margaret were his star pupils when it came to playing the cornet. He had started them both when they were quite young back in Great Britain. Although Alice was older, Margaret showed a more natural ability on the cornet.

Otis gladly took up his work at Pick-Penn Iron & Smelting Works and was soon well acquainted with the other bandsmen and their families. It was a common weekend pastime for the band to play at the Pick-Penn Family Park where the company had a place for workers to picnic. Management knew that it was good for morale to sponsor the band. It also built better team spirit among the employees and helped the immigrant workers to feel a part of their new country.

This also gave the families time together away from the city. Pick-Penn utilized the PRT to move their employees to the company park. The company hired the street cars so the rides were free. Once at the park, families would enjoy the band concert and then have a picnic lunch that they either brought from home, or they could purchase tasty treats from some of the park booths. Sarsparilla or root beer drinks could be had for a few cents. Frankfurters were popular among the Germans. They especially liked the Thuringer sausage with Dusseldorf mustard and those tiny rolls that were nothing more than a handle. Sandwiches and potato salad of various kinds could be seen when the families gathered to eat.

Otis had always wanted to try his hand at rowing one of the little red and white boats on the lagoon. One day he convinced Sara to go for a ride with him. Margaret and Alice watched as Otis helped their mother into the little wooden boat by the pier. It was a little tippy and they all laughed heartily at the contortions it took to get into the boat. Then Otis gingerly stepped on to the rower's seat, causing the boat to tip about and their mother to scream with school-girl delight. He pushed off from the pier and took the oars, Sara waved at the girls and said, "Behave while we are gone."

These were the last words they ever heard from their mother or father. At the end of the day as families were beginning to pack up and head for the PRT and home, Alice and Margaret began looking for their parents. Some of the men from the band started to help and took a rowboat out on the lagoon to look for them. All they found was an overturned boat.

It was presumed that they were drowned, but the other workers did not tell Alice and Margaret this news. Families were sent home and Alice and Margaret went with their next door neighbors, the Hintzes. Pick-Penn owners called in the police, but it was too dark to search that night. The next day at dawn the search began and Sara's and Otis's bodies were found. Pick-Penn employee's took up a collection to help pay for the funerals and the company paid for the remainder.

♫

So Alice and Margaret worked together to survive in their new country. Alice, being the oldest, was offered a job at the factory and Margaret doubled her efforts in school. She was determined to help her sister as soon as she was old enough to work. In fact, she was very good at numbers and loved to play with various equations and would show this to Alice after dinner most evenings.

One evening she said, "Alice, we should start our own company. We would be better off in business by ourselves."

"Margaret, what do you know of business? What would the good people at Pick-Penn think of us? It would look like we were ungrateful if I were to leave the factory, and what if we failed?

Then how would we put food on our table and a roof over our heads?"

But Margaret would not be dissuaded. She could see the plan taking shape in her head. "I can set this all up if I stop school for a while. We just have to find the thing that people will pay money for and that will fit our skills."

Alice wasn't sure about this business of business, but she let her sister talk and they brought up ideas of what they could do. By bedtime it was decided that they could sew something. The questions was, sew what?

The next day Alice went off to her factory work, a little lighter of step, humming the lyrical strain to Arthur Pryor's new trombone solo, *Thoughts of Love*. She hoped that Margaret could come up with an idea. Margaret was always good at this sort of thing and it might mean she wouldn't have to work all of those long hours at the factory. She hoped to find a beau and to get married, but that didn't seem possible now unless Margaret could really make those numbers work.

For her part, Margaret began her day by walking through her neighborhood. She did a little shopping for their evening meal and decided to talk to the shopkeepers to ask what people would buy. Things were looking glum until she entered Leutzinger's Dry Goods Store. It was empty in mid morning and Mr. Leutzinger was reading the morning edition of the Philadelphia Tribune newspaper. He set the newspaper down on the top of the glass display case and smiled at Margaret. "Well, Miss Blackthorn, how are you today?" He still had a thick accent from his Swiss homeland.

"I am very well, Mr. Leutzinger, thank you. How are you?"

"I am fine. I was just reading in the morning paper that our city will be hosting the centennial celebration of the United States. What do you think of that?" He bounced as he talked and his bushy eyebrows bounced right along too.

Margaret looked at the news article and saw a photo with President Ulysses S. Grant announcing the event for July 4, 1876, just a little more than a year hence. There it was, a platform covered with red, white and blue bunting. Margaret knew what they must sew. She turned on her heel and called over her shoulder "Good day, Mr. Leutzinger."

"Did you need something from the store?"

"Thank you Mr. Leutzinger, I have it!"

She nearly forgot that a proper lady should not run in her desire to get home. The thoughts were beginning to come together in her mind. Once back in their little flat she prepared raw fried potatoes. Margaret always thought well when cooking. She washed a few potatoes and sliced them thinly. In her black cast iron skillet she fried up the potatoes. As they became sumptuously brown she removed them to a side platter and covered them with another plate to keep them warm. The skillet had been her mother's and she took great pride in using it. Next she took out the bacon ends and set to frying them in the skillet. As the bacon crisped up she removed it to the platter as well. When Alice came home from work she would make a bacon gravy by stirring in flour and then adding the potatoes and bacon back in. They would savor this meal because soon she would have to forgo purchasing bacon so she could afford to buy cloth. She whistled away at Pat Gilmore's *Dinner Bell Polka*. When Alice came in, she recounted her day and the plans for their new company. She even had a name picked out: "Blackthorne Bunting Works".

"Do you really think this can work? How will you do your banking? That's all man's work. Will any business man work with you, a mere girl?" Alice was distressed, and yet there was excitement in her voice.

"Well, if we don't try, what will our future be? I shall appeal to their sense of patriotism. Let me try it, Alice. That's all I ask."

Alice thought it over while Margaret showed her the numbers on the back of an old paper sack. She knew Margaret would be persistent and frankly, she was too tired to argue with her. "Go ahead. I probably wouldn't be able to talk you out of it anyway."

So the next day Margaret went around to the stores where she normally shopped and began asking for storeowners to adorn their shops with red, white and blue bunting that she and her sister would sew. They would be specially made to fit the front windows of their establishments. Mr. Leutzinger was her first customer. He agreed to a deposit of half down and the other half to be paid upon delivery of the bunting. It was hard to resist this enthusiastic young woman.

The deposit made it possible to purchase the fabric and thread. She already had scissors, needles and thimble in her modest sewing basket. At dinner she was able to share her success. Alice was pleased, but thought that bouncy Mr. Leutzinger had just taken pity on two orphan girls.

♫

The next day Margaret set out to measure Mr. Leutzinger's windows. With measurements in hand she purchased the fabric. At home she created a pattern, cut the pieces and began sewing. In three days she delivered the new bunting to Leutzinger's Dry Goods Store.

"May I help you hang these bunting on your windows, Mr. Leutzinger? You'll be the first merchant on the street to show your patriotism! I can hold the bunting up while you nail the top band to the window sill." He got a hammer and some nails and the new bunting was soon secured. Shoppers commented right away on how beautiful the decorations looked.

Margaret crossed the street to the bank. This was the employee bank for Pick-Penn Smelting & Iron Works. Margaret asked politely to see the bank president. After a few minutes wait he came out of his office to see her and was about to invite her into his office. He had known Otis and was well aware of the Blackthorne girl's situation. "Mr. Treeder, would you come outside with me? I'd like to show you something."

He was a little surprised, but nodded his assent. On the front sidewalk Margaret pointed out the beautiful bunting across the street. She detailed her plan and then said, "Surely the Pick-Penn Bank will want to show its patriotic pride with bunting as well." And she got an order from Mr. Treeder.

Soon the orders came in without asking. Margaret needed more people to sew. She asked the wives of some of the Pick-Penn bandsmen. Alice was able to quit her job at the Pick-Penn factory to work toward making the Blackthorne Bunting Works a real business, but she hated sewing.

"Margaret, let's switch jobs. I'll keep house and you run your business."

"It's *our* business, Alice! The Blackthorne name is on it."

"I don't want to run a business! I would like to have a beau and get married!"

"You can't run a business and be married?"

"No proper gentleman is going to court a lady who is trying to compete with him in business!"

"That's silly! Why would he care?"

"What kind of wife and mother would you be if you were always thinking about business? What kind of man would want a wife who worked with complex numbers?"

"A good one!"

"A good one what?" She was exasperated with Margaret - never following convention, always asking why.

"Both answers. A good wife and mother and a good man."

"I'll work with you, Margaret, but I don't want the responsibility of the business around my neck. That's yours!"

So they had come to an agreement. Under Margaret's persistent sales work the business boomed. Alice was even able to attend some of the "coming out parties" of the daughters of the managers of Pick-Penn Smelting & Iron Works. Now that Blackthorne Bunting Works was the largest purveyor of bunting in the state of Pennsylvania and beyond she could be considered as marriageable to some of the socially prominent young men in the city.

One Saturday evening she was introduced to a young doctor, James Tudor. James was from Baltimore, Maryland. His father had been a doctor who studied in Paris, France. James' father, Dr. Albert Henry Tudor, came to America and set up his practice. He did just that. He met and married Claire Mae Taveen and they had a bouncing baby son, James Henry. Then came the Civil War. Albert thought it important to serve his new country and enlisted in the Union army. He was a surgeon at the Battle of Antietam. Working with the wounded was very hard work and he eventually contracted an illness and died. Fellow officers saw to it that Claire and her son were taken care of. She married Major Howard Francis Darby after the war and James was brought up like his own son.

James matriculated from Harvard Medical School and established his practice in Baltimore. He was in Philadelphia visiting one of his medical school friends when he met Alice. He swept her off her feet and they were married in short order. The happy couple removed to Baltimore where they set up their home.

Margaret was thrilled for her sister and she loved her new brother-in-law. But Alice was afraid to have her sister visit her in Baltimore. She was ashamed to introduce Margaret to her social circle. What would the genteel ladies of her new home think of businesswoman Margaret? So they agreed to stay in touch, but they also agreed that Margaret would concentrate on her work while Alice began her new life. Margaret focused on growing her business and it flourished. Eventually she had over six hundred people working for her. Many of her stitchers were the wives of some of the Pick-Penn Company bandsmen.

♫

Margaret Blackthorne, having made her fortune, now dedicated herself to the improvement of ladies through band music. She heard the celebrated band of Helen May Butler: "The Female Sousa," and felt empowered to conduct a band of her own. Though it was not generally acceptable for ladies to play musical instruments other than the piano, patriotic band music was sweeping the country with the emergence of John Philip Sousa and His Band. So even the ladies were now joining in the fun of this very American music.

There were people in some areas of Philadelphia where Miss Blackthorne was considered "uppity". They thought that the ladies in the band were wasting their time. They thought that young ladies should devote themselves to singing or piano or perhaps the violin, but certainly not a wind instrument where they would contort their lovely features.

As rehearsal ended, the ladies chatted excitedly about their new band piece *Cake Walk*, a schottishe by George Southwell, and the progress the whole band was making. Miss Blackthorne had pronounced their rehearsal a stunning success. She was certain that their performance for the Ladies Auxiliary to the Benjamin Franklin Free Thinkers Society cake walk would be met with rousing approval.

Poor Christina was swabbing out her piccolo, checking the keys to see if a spring was loose or a pad was no longer seated properly. It leaked somewhere and just wouldn't play. Clearly she would have to visit the C.G. Conn music store to have it fixed.

Vashti put away her horn and sprang to Christina's side. "Will you take your piccolo to the Conn store tomorrow?" She asked with all the anticipation of a Grand Pause.

"I *imagine* so."

"You'll need someone to go with you – yes?"

"I *imagine* so," Christina said with a knowing smile. Jack O'Brien would be at the music store and Christina was having a little fun with Vashti. Jack was Vashti's beau and was even allowed to call on her at the Smith home. Christina could easily arrange to have Vashti come along so Jack would be surprised, but she was clearly making a game of it.

"Christina, I don't know why I bother talking to you!" Vashti blurted stamping her beautiful tan high button shoes in an exquisite *sfzorzando*.

"It's because you have designs on that unusual Jack O'Brien. I don't know what you see in him, Vashti. He's not a very good musician and he doesn't appear to read or want to better himself. What is it about that young man that you find so fascinating?"

Vashti thought for a moment about the kind-hearted Jack. He wasn't a great musician, but he loved all things mechanical and was always tinkering with his ophicleide to see if he could make its sound stronger. Many bandsmen considered the ophicleide to be an outmoded instrument. The much louder tuba and recently invented Sousaphone carried the bass line magnificently in any group, but Jack stuck with his beloved ophicleide.

Though not a great musician, Jack was a great dancer. He had rhythm in his feet and studied the latest ragtime dances. At local social club dances he was a sight to behold and all the girls wanted to dance with him. "He's a wonderful dancer!" was Vashti's reply.

"Do you really think that is a characteristic that signals matrimony?"

Sadie had walked over during this conversation and had surmised that they were talking about Jack.

Vasthi continued, "He's a snappy dresser. Just think of the beautiful children we would have!" This made Sadie all dewy-eyed. She was a pushover for cute children.

"Vashti! You have barely known that boy for six months. Don't you think it's a little forward of you to have imagined marriage and children?" chortled Christina.

Coming back to reality, Vashti replied, "Well, then, he's very good with his hands. It would be good to have someone mechanical around the house." Vashti looked at Christina who blushed a high pink in her cheeks and they all dissolved into fits of laughter.

When they had regained their composure, Christina said, "I *imagine* that you could accompany me to the music store tomorrow. Do you want to come as well, Sadie? Maybe we could make a morning of it and do a little shopping as well."

Danforth had returned, bursting with excitement after his evening of billiards. Christina and Sadie joined Amanda Fetkenheuer and her mother for their ride home. In only a few minutes the Great Hall was empty and Miss Blackthorne could focus her attention on gathering her music together. She had always been meticulous about her work, be it learning the cornet as a child or sewing her bunting. Later, her tidy, smart way of dressing showed her concern, and the loving care of the women musicians under her tutelage in the Betsy Ross All-Lady Silver Cornet Band was known to everyone.

Stanley Robertson, Miss Blackthorne's driver, was waiting patiently for her to complete her work. Then he would bring the handsome blue carriage with the Blackthorne Bunting Works crest on its door up to the door and drive Miss Blackthorne home. It had been his privilege to do this for nearly twenty years now and he was devoted to this wonderful lady.

Stanley Robertson was a freed slave. Coming north to Philadelphia, he had first found work at the Blackthorne Bunting Works sweeping floors. Miss Blackthorne never looked down on him because he had been a slave any more than she thought women couldn't work and better themselves. For this kindness to him, he became a devoted employee and had risen through various jobs at the Works to become the top driver.

“I’m ready, Stanley. Please bring the carriage up.”

“Right away, Miss Blackthorne.”

After a few minutes the sleek blue carriage came up to the door pulled by a matched pair of bays. Margaret loved those horses, but she thought that the day was fast approaching when she would need to switch over to the PRT. For now she could climb into the carriage, sink into the soft leather seat and relax on her way home. She always put every ounce of energy into the rehearsals and at the end knew she had given her all. She was looking forward to getting home to relax.

Stepping out of the stage door, she walked to the carriage where Stanley was holding the door of the carriage for her. “Home, Stanley, but do spare the horses.” Closing her eyes she listened to the gentle clop of the horses hooves on the cobblestone.

# Chapter 2

The next day, Vashti and her mother took the PRT to Sadie's house to pick her up for their downtown excursion. With Sadie safely in tow, the next stop was to Christina Swenson's. Vashti loved to pound the door knocker at Swenson's. It was a beautiful wrought iron decorative lion. The face looked out at you and the body was seated with the tasseled tail working as the knocker. Mrs. Swenson had domestic help and Rosalie, the Irish cook, answered the door.

"Good mornin' t'ya, Mrs. Smith, Miss Vashti and Miss Sadie. Miss Christina is nearly ready. Won't you come into the parlor to wait for her?" asked Rosalie in her lilting Irish brogue.

"I will go and see how long Miss Christina will be. Would anyone like a cup of tea first?" Rosalie offered. The ladies declined her offer and sat down in the well-complemented room while Rosalie padded off, intent on her mission.

"This is such a lovely room," Mrs. Smith said admiringly. "I want the two of you girls to study the way this room is organized. Someday you will each live in a home with a parlor like this. This will be the room where you will entertain your lady friends when they come by to visit. Look at the way this room is decorated. How would you decorate your parlor? What colors would you use?

"I would use lots of reds and yellows in my parlor," Sadie offered.

"Red and yellow, catch a fellow!" quipped Vashti and they all laughed warmly. I'd use a very warm, pink, rose color. I just love the tea service that you have, Mother, and I would have colors that would complement a set just like yours." Vashti beamed at her mother.

"Mrs. Smith, how did you learn so much about domestic science?"

"Well Sadie, I learned some of it from my mother, but you know that I love to read, so I was a devotee of *Godey's Magazine and*

*Lady's Book.* A wonderful lady by the name of Sarah Josepha Hale was the editor. She was known to be quite the arbiter of good taste. I followed her advice very closely. Each and every issue came with a full color fashion-plate."

Elizabeth was warming to the subject. She would clench her hands together in tight little fists and shake them in tiny circles near her chin. Her cheeks were flushed and her voice was rising in pitch.

"Didn't you tell me once that there was music in those magazines as well?"

"Yes, daughter, I did. The latest polka, waltz or gallop was printed inside. I was not much of a pianist, but my friends learned each new piece so they could entertain at their parlor pianos."

"I don't know how I could use my tuba to entertain!" Again they laughed good-naturedly.

"Oh Sadie, you will have your afternoon tea there and perhaps there will be plays read aloud, or the latest poetry. Godey's published great authors like Edgar Allen Poe." She turned toward her daughter, "Vashti, your father would read the stories of Edgar Allen Poe when he came to call on me. Or you might even play cards there. Cards are not so greatly frowned upon these days."

Sadie's head bobbled as Elisabeth spoke. "Do you still have some of those magazines, Mrs. Smith? I would like to read one."

"I'll have to look, Sadie. I think I still do. It isn't published anymore, but I believe I saved my copies and they are somewhere in our attic."

Christina made her entrance to the parlor, followed by her mother. Mrs. Swenson had been busy braiding Christina's hair and then winding it around the top of her head like a crown. Her golden locks were nearly the color of a lacquered band instrument. With her lovely blue eyes and statuesque height, she was quite the beauty. Mrs. Swenson was just a slightly older version, and you could certainly tell they were mother and daughter.

Mrs. Swenson didn't speak English very well. She only understood it when spoken slowly and if the speaker used very simple words. She smiled softly and offered her hand to Mrs. Smith with a simple, "Gud Morning". Mrs. Smith took her fingertips and smiled a good morning to her as well.

Christina spoke to her mother in Swedish. After a short conversation Christina said, "We can go now." They headed to the front door, a little group of ladies intent on a morning of shopping. Rosalie was already at the door and they mouthed their goodbyes to Mrs. Swenson.

Rosalie called, "G'day, ladies," and closed the doors behind them as they walked down the front steps, turned right and walked two blocks to the PRT.

♫

Vashti thought nothing in the world could possibly be as dazzling as a musical instrument store. She knew that the others enjoyed visiting C.G. Conn Co., but they would have other places more exciting to them. Her mother would want to stop by Mrs. Weatherbee's Millinery shop to see the latest fashions in hats. Margaret Weatherbee was always happy to work with her customers to help them update a hat from the last season or the season before. Most of her customers were respectable middle class ladies who kept current with their mode of dress, but were also careful about the family budget. Vashti's mother would have a pleasurable conversation about ribbons and lace. She would likely bring her brown hat in the next time she was in the area to have it updated for the fall.

Sadie would be happy to visit each store, to look at hats and to try a few of them on. She would gaze at the tubas at Conn but her mouth was already watering for salt-water taffy. Christina would drop off her piccolo to be fixed. She would look at the latest sheet music and admire shiny instruments. Then she would look forward to visiting Harberger Booksellers.

Vashti could be content spending the entire day at Conn's. It was like a candy store for musicians, and she had first met Jack O'Brien at the store. He had started working there three years ago as an errand boy. If the latest flyers for new flutes were ready, he would walk to pick up the flyers. When Olson Dreyers brought shipments of musical instruments in wooden crates, he gingerly helped to unload them so they wouldn't get dented. Using a wheeled dollie, he would roll these boxes into the center of the store where they were stacked for all to see and to create wonderment at what was inside. This little bit of showmanship guaranteed that folks would return to the store often to see what new instruments were added to the sales cases.

Musicians young and old came to the store to see the latest models. The elegance of the display cases, made of the finest oak, perfectly set off the musical treasures inside. One case held Four-in-One cornets, Vocal cornets and the coveted Wonder cornet. In another were Artist's Model trombones, Wonder Double-wall clarinets, Howe Wonder Model flutes and yet another held various sized drums. On the walls hung helicon basses. Conn had them all. Here was a store where the members of John Philip Sousa's band came to choose their instruments and to have them repaired as well.

Nearly everyone started on a beginner instrument and then purchased a new instrument that was a step up from their first model when they had attained a higher level of skill. The store would take used instruments in trade toward a newer model. The older instrument would be cleaned and given a thorough going over before it was returned to the sales floor. Daniel O'Toole, who was the Master Woodwind Repairman at the Conn store, was teaching Jack the repair trade. Jack had been working long enough with the repairmen that he was often allowed to work on these older instruments.

The O'Toole and O'Brien families had known each other for years. They were all members of St. Patrick's Catholic Church and lived in the same neighborhood. Daniel O'Toole was a widower. His wife

Mary had died in childbirth a number of years ago. The child, a son, lived just under a week. Daniel lost himself in his work and in playing clarinet with the Sons of Killarney Band. He didn't marry again and had no other children. Daniel was invited to dinner at the O'Brien house every Sunday after Mass. Jack proved to be very mechanical and they developed a close bond. Daniel was able to get him into the Killarney Band where he played an old ophicleide. Eventually Daniel spoke to Mr. Arthur Ritberger, the owner of the Conn Store, about Jack. Mr. Ritberger knew Daniel to be an honest, hardworking man and brought Jack in with the idea of him becoming an apprentice to Daniel. Both men could see the skill that Jack had with the repair tools and it seemed an unspoken fact that Jack would eventually take Daniel's place.

Jack observed that the boys' bands often had older instruments to start on. For example, all of the brass players would start out on the cornet. If they proved to have a lip for the cornet, they would stay on that instrument. If they didn't do well on the cornet they would move to another brass instrument with a larger mouthpiece, going ever larger, alto horn to tenor horn to baritone to tuba until the perfect fit was found.

This proved a very successful approach since all the popular brass instruments used the same fingering system. Each had three valves in a row. Valve number one lowered the pitch by one whole step. Valve number two lowered a note a half step, and the third valve was a combination of the other two, lowering notes a step and a half. By using various valve combinations, one could attain any pitch.

Vashti enjoyed hearing Jack talk about the technical aspects of his work. They would sit in the parlor sipping Ceylon tea with honey and Jack would talk about how instruments were made. Sometimes he had little scraps of brown paper where he had sketched dimensions of woodwind keys and the size and shape of things like clarinet bells. He was so passionate about these concepts that everyone would be caught up in the excitement. Vashti's father and mother knew that their daughter had a good head on her shoulders and encouraged her to learn arithmetic and number skills. She was never intimidated by Jack's technical conversations.

♫

The quartet of ladies entered the C.G. Conn store through an ornate brass framed revolving door. Vashti loved these doors and as a child would often push her way around more than once. Inside the store, the pungent aroma of valve oil, slide cream and key oil tickled her nostrils. Vashti thought these scents to be even better than the fanciest French perfume, but she kept that thought to herself.

The smells in the store brought to mind the first day that each of the girls came into the store with Miss Blackthorne to buy their instruments. Essence of lubricants brought back that magical moment. Since there were no girls' bands in Philadelphia before Miss Blackthorne started the Betsy Ross All-Lady Silver Cornet Band, it was necessary to purchase new instruments. There was no inventory of older cornets like the boys' bands.

Miss Blackthorne brought the girls in to the Conn store in small groups. Because she was a well respected member of the community and a highly successful business woman, various mercantile establishments were happy to do business with her as she always paid her bills on time, even though it was a bit unusual for a woman to engage in business.
She had an idea of the instrument each young lady would play, but she devoted time to each budding musician to help her find a good match. Vashti, Sadie, Christina, Amanda Fetkenheuer and Cybil Hayes were among the young ladies to start with the band. If they weren't able to pay for their instruments outright, the Blackthorne Bunting Works would pay for the instrument and the family could pay the company as they were able. Vashti suspected that Miss Blackthorne actually bought the instruments for some of the young ladies whose families would have found it difficult if not impossible to afford even a used instrument. This was never spoken of when the band began to practice together. If Miss Blackthorne had said it once, she had said it a million times, "Ladies, there are no unimportant parts. The band needs you all to play well."

Mr. and Mrs. Smith were thrilled to have Vashti in the band. They liked Miss Blackthorne and respected her work in the community.

They wanted great role models for their daughter. Richard and Elizabeth had encouraged all of the Smith children to try new things and to step outside of traditional roles. They wanted Vashti to associate with people from other backgrounds. They liked her band friends, Jack with his inventive diagrams and Miss Blackthorne with her entrepreneurial spirit. The new century was coming quickly and they wanted their children to enter it with a progressive American spirit.

Christina made her way to the counter where Mr. Ritberger greeted her warmly. Mr. Ritberger didn't always remember names, but he knew Christina was one of the young ladies in Miss Blackthorne's band. The fifty new instruments he had sold to that new band were a tremendous boon to his business. "Hello, Miss. How may I help you today?"

"Good morning, Mr. Ritberger. I am Christina Swenson. I am the piccolo player in the Betsy Ross All-Lady Silver Cornet Band. I'm having trouble with my piccolo. Would you please take a look at it?" She brought the petite piccolo out of her brocade handbag and handed it to Mr. Ritberger.

Sadie watched this exchange with interest. She would never be able to carry her instrument in her handbag, but while Christina was the proverbial cherry on the top of the sundae, Sadie and the other tuba ladies were the foundation of the band. "It's all right," thought Sadie. "There are no unimportant parts."

Mr. Ritberger put the two joints of the piccolo together and blew over the tone hole on the lip plate. He was a fair flute player and piccolo was similar to flute. He was able to diagnose the problem.

"Well, Miss Swenson, I can tell that one of the pads isn't closing all of the way. I see that you are here with friends. Have you more business to attend to in the city this morning?"

"Thank you, Mr. Ritberger. My friends and I have made plans to do a bit of shopping this morning." She gave him a charming smile.

"I will have my woodwind man, Mr. O'Toole, look at it and have it ready for you in an hour. Oh, Mrs. Tudor, would you be so kind as to take Miss Swenson's piccolo back to Mr. O'Toole?"

Mrs. Tudor drifted by, gently taking the piccolo case from her boss. "Certainly, Mr. Ritberger."

Mrs. Smith had arrived at the counter too. She reached out her gloved hand and Mr. Ritberger took it delicately in his fingertips. "Good day to you, Mr. Ritberger. I am Mrs. Richard Smith."

At the mention of her husband's name, his eyes shown a little brighter. "And a hearty good morning to you, ma'am.

"Mr. Ritberger, we will be about our day and will return in approximately one hour and a half for Miss Swenson's piccolo. I believe that you and I will have some additional business at that time. Yes?"

"Yes, Mrs. Smith, we will indeed." He said with a broad smile on his face.

"Mother! You don't mean to tell me that…"

" Hush, Vashti," Mrs. Smith interrupted. "We can discuss this later."

Vashti had been looking for Jack. She had caught a glimpse of him carrying a stack of clarinet cases down the hall. She didn't actually see his face, but she knew the shoes that he always wore. After tinkering with the mechanics on musical instruments, dancing was a favorite pastime for Jack O'Brien and he always wore fancy shoes to show off his footwork. Jack was so proud of his shoes that he employed eight-year-old Seamus O'Flarrity to polish his shoes. He would leave them in the hallway just outside the O'Brien door. Seamus would pick them up late in the evening and have them spit shined and ready the next morning for Jack to wear. This cost Jack five cents a week, but it was worth it.

There was no doubt that he was there, but she would have to wait until later to see him. She hadn't been able to warn him that they were coming, but he would very likely see Christina's piccolo and know that they would be back. Both he and Daniel O'Toole knew every woodwind and most of the brass instruments that came through their shop. Those instruments were their own calling card. Each one had a serial number that identified it. Daniel kept meticulous notes on repairs on 3x5 cards that he kept in a special file near his workbench.

Christina had watched Vashti's gaze and said, "I *imagine* you will be more successful later." They both laughed.

"Thank you, Mr. Ritberger," said Mrs. Smith. "We'll all be back later."

"You are welcome, ladies. Have a pleasant morning." They all thanked him and said good-bye as they traced their steps to the front of the store, past the cases filled with beautiful brass basses and silver double-chamber Boehm system clarinets. Through the brass door they revolved their way out to the sidewalk and into the sunshine.

"Mother! Has Miss Blackthorne's cornet come into the store?" blurted Vashti.

"Hush, my daughter, and you as well, Sadie and Christina. We don't want to spoil the surprise. Last evening while you were at band practice, that nice young man Jack O'Brien brought a message to our home. We would have come in to the store today to get the cornet anyway. Christina's piccolo problem just gave us a good excuse to be at the store. We want to keep the secret, don't we?" She raised her eyebrows questioningly. "We won't discuss this anymore, lest someone overhear us along the sidewalk."

"Agreed!" said Vashti while Christina nodded and Sadie, dewy-eyed, bobbled her head.

They made their rounds to Mrs. Weatherbee's hat shop and then to Harberger's Booksellers, then finally to Lafleuer's Confectioners where Sadie was able to get her salt-water taffy. Lafleuers didn't always have her favorite flavor, strawberry. Sometimes they didn't have taffy either. The temperature had to be just right to make the taffy and to bring it into the city from the seaside so that it didn't melt into a glob of goo. Sadie bought a small bag and immediately said, "I'll be happy to share."

Mrs. Smith walked with the young ladies to a small park with benches that was on the way back to the Conn store. When seated, Sadie offered each of her friends a piece of candy, which they eagerly accepted. Then she offered one to Mrs. Smith as well who said, "No, thank you, Sadie. I'm trying to keep my hourglass figure. You enjoy it."

The happy quartet sat in the shade enjoying a short rest watching the people pass by. There were children playing in the park and mothers with babies in their prams out for their morning airing. Across the street they could hear the strains of a Sousa march coming from a Victrola. It was Sousa's *Washington Post March* played on piano. One could hardly walk a block in the city without hearing Sousa's music coming from a Victrola or being played on a piano. Mr. Sousa was incredibly famous and the members of the Betsy Ross All-Lady Silver Cornet Band deemed it a true sign of accomplishment to be playing his music.

Elisabeth broke the silence. "When we get back to the store, take care that you say nothing about the cornet. We don't know who else will be in the store and this must continue to be a secret."

They rose in unison and walked back. It was a short walk completed with a spring in their steps. Arriving back at the store, they revolved their way into the sales floor where there were a dozen or so people looking at instruments. Mr. Ritberger was helping a man who was looking at Saxophones. Vashti caught Jack's eye. He was standing at the ready in the frame of the door that led to the repair rooms and his cheeks were flushed with excitement. Though she hoped he was excited about seeing her, she was pretty sure it was more about the cornet. Vashti knew she had risen above dancing in Jack's evaluation, but she wasn't sure she could ever be more important to him than things musical and mechanical.

Jack was watching Mr. Ritberger who now motioned to him to bring the piccolo up from the repair room. He executed a sharp about face and was off to the back of the building. Very shortly he returned carrying the beautiful little black case. Christina met him by the cash register. Mr. Ritberger was there to make the sale and asked Jack to go back and work with the man who was looking at Saxophones.

"Well, Miss Swenson, Mr. O'Toole did a nice job for you. Just as I thought, one of the pads was not seating properly. He replaced the pad and made sure everything was in proper adjustment." He rang the sale up on the cash register. Like everything else in the store, it was fancy with its Tiffany styled case and shiny brass-lacquer. The new pad and the work cost 15 cents. Christina took this from her handbag and paid Mr. Ritberger. Then he motioned to Mrs. Smith to follow him to his office. The ladies waited in the store.

Walking down the hallway just a short distance, they came to a dark wooden door with an etched glass window on which were placed gold leaf letters pronouncing OFFICE. The etching was of C.G. Conn. At the top were the words "Largest Band Instrument Manufactory in the United States." In the center was a round frame with a likeness of Mr. Conn in the middle. A stunning cornet was etched below the portrait bordered on one side by Pan with his pipes and on the other by a testimonial. The bottom was framed with "C.G. Conn, Proprietor, Elkhart, Indiana, U.S.A".

Mr. Ritberger opened the door to reveal three steps up into his office. The wood was smooth and shiny as Mrs. Smith took hold of the front of her skirt to ascend the steps. The office was filled with light as there were windows on three sides. This allowed Mr. Ritberger to look out over the sales floor to see if he were needed to assist with a sale.

"This is a lovely office, Mr. Ritberger!" As was her custom, Elisabeth studied the way everything was decorated.

"Thank you, Mrs. Smith. I am here at the store a great deal of time, so I like to have a well-appointed office."

The room had beautiful wood bookcases that matched the large, exquisitely carved mahogany desk with a green leather chair behind it. On the desk sat a blotter, two gold fountain pens in a brass holder, a humidor presumably filled with cigars and a square ashtray that had a view of the Conn factory in the center. There was also a brass lamp with a green shade and a pull chain. Towards the windows in the front of the room was a round table with chairs. They all matched the mahogany of the desk and the chairs had green inlaid leather seats with a scrolling design worked into the leather. The table had a red velvet tablecloth that just covered the top. In the center was a black leather case with a leather handle that had brass buckles attaching it to the case.

Elizabeth walked over the red, black and gold Oriental rug, gazed at the case and held her breath. Mr. Ritberger came up behind her and opened the latches. As he slowly lifted the top of the case they could both smell the newness of the leather, the newly oiled valves and the slides that were recently greased. Then the ornately engraved cornet caught the light. “It’s just beautiful!” Elizabeth clasped her hands over her heart. She had no idea that the presentation cornet would be such a work of art and she was speechless.

“We are so pleased to have been able to fill your order for this cornet. The Conn band instruments are really without equal, ma’am.”

“It’s so intricately adorned,” said Elisabeth, slightly breathless with emotion. Her gloved hand reached out to the horn and gently touched the engraving on the bell.

“Do you expect to have this cornet presented to Miss Blackthorne at the cakewalk this weekend? I would be happy to be there for the presentation.”

Elisabeth was still stunned at the artistic beauty of the instrument. She was quite overwhelmed and knew this would be thrill for Miss Blackthorne. When she regained her composure she said, “I do believe that it will be presented this weekend, Mr. Ritberger. My husband is the head of the committee and he can contact you with the final details. He will be one of the presenters. I believe he was in earlier this morning to pay you the remainder due. I am just to bring it home with me."

"Very well, Mrs. Smith. I have had Mr. O'Toole, our master craftsman, check over the work of Bruno Stein, our Master Brass Repairman." Mr. Ritberger closed the cornet case carefully, clasped the shiny brass latches and picked up the case. "I'll have this wrapped nicely for you, Mrs. Smith. Please have a seat and wait right here. I'll be just a moment. I could have a cup of tea brought in for you if you like."

"No, thank you, Mr. Ritberger. I think I'll just want to take the cornet home. The fewer people who see us with that package, the better chance we have of keeping the secret."

He nodded and went out of the office, turning toward the back of the store. In the back was a large room where instruments were unpacked from their crates and extra stock was stored. Ritberger walked over to a utilitarian table where there was a large bolt of brown paper on a spindle that allowed it to be pulled out for wrapping things. As he set the cornet on the table he heard the soft step of Mrs. Tudor. "I can wrap that for you, Mr. Ritberger."

"Thank you, Mrs. Tudor. Be sure to attach a wood carrying handle to the outside with twine. Mrs. Smith will be carrying it to her home on the PRT."

Mrs. Tudor had been working in the store for about six months. He didn't know much about her, but a telegram had come from Mr. C.G. Conn himself asking Ritberger to offer her a job in his store. She was a very good worker, always on time, polite and tidy in her appearance, but she never smiled. Her face, on the infrequent occasions when she would look up carried the lines of one who had lived a hard life. He didn't think she had reached the age of 40 yet, but he didn't ask too many questions, especially ones concerning a lady's age. That simply wasn't done in polite society. One day she just presented herself at the store asking for him. She introduced herself and asked if he might have some work for her to do. It did not matter if it was menial. She would be happy of any small job. So he hired her to do dusting, filing of music and light work in the store. He knew this would garner him some good favor with the Conn Co. and was careful to send a telegram back to Mr. Conn when she had been hired.

Jack entered the back room. "Mr. Ritberger, a shipment of new soprano saxophones has arrived. Would you like them brought back here?"

"Yes, Jack. Have the deliveryman put them in the center of the room and you can inventory them later. Then they will go up on the shelves here," he said, pointing to the saxophone section of their storage area. "Thank you, Jack."

Turning his attention to the cornet, he saw that Mrs. Tudor had finished wrapping it. She attached a handle and handed it to Mr. Ritberger. "Thank you, Mrs. Tudor," he said as he spun on his heel and walked briskly back to his office. Opening the door, he went up the three steps and smiled at Mrs. Smith. "Here you are, ma'am. I had a nice handle attached to help you. You'll be alright carrying it?"

"Thank you, Mr. Ritberger. I have my daughter, who is used to carrying a French horn, and her friend, Miss Thomas, who readily carries a tuba. We'll manage just fine." She shook his hand. He saw her back out to the sales floor where the three girls gathered. They revolved their way back onto the sidewalk, made their way to the PRT and dropped each one of the young ladies off in reverse order, finally arriving back at the Smith home just in time to put the cornet in Richard's study and freshen up a bit for lunch.

# Chapter 3

Thursday and Friday couldn't possibly have dragged on more slowly. The anticipation of the Ladies Auxiliary to the Benjamin Franklin Free Thinker's Society cakewalk was almost too much for Vashti to bear. The added excitement of the presentation of the silver cornet to Miss Blackthorne only added to the anticipation. It pained her that she could tell no one, but she also knew this was for the best. It must be kept a secret.

Finally Friday afternoon came and Vashti could think about getting her uniform out of the tall cherry wood wardrobe in her bedroom. The uniforms were a wonder. Miss Blackthorne had seen the all-female band of Helen May Butler: The Female Sousa. She was an inspiration for thousands of lady musicians wherever she and her band traveled. Miss Butler modeled her band after John Philip Sousa's band. Her ladies wore dark blue military style band caps with musical lyre symbols on the top. They wore long dark blue skirts that had black piping down the front to accent the panels in the skirts. Each musician wore a starched, brilliantly white shirtwaist with a charming dark blue ribbon clasped at the throat by a pin in the shape of a circle fashioned of baby pearls.

When Miss Blackthorne worked on the uniform design for the Betsy Ross All-Lady Silver Cornet Band, she wanted uniforms that were the height of fashion and flattering to the shape of all her musicians. The skirts were made of beautifully woven cotton broad cloth. A pattern of red pin stripes ran vertically in the blue fabric. The jacket was a fashionable military style in navy blue. There were rows of brass buttons down each side that fastened a placket across the front. The brass buttons had two crossed flags on them. At the shoulder, where the sleeves met the main body of the coat, there was an embroidered emblem showing the two crossed flags. One was the original flag sewn by Betsy Ross with a circle of thirteen white stars and the other was the current flag of the United States with forty-five stars. Below the flags was a display of cascading Blackthorne bunting. The jacket sleeves had a row of three smaller flag buttons and the waist of the jacket was shaped into a peplum with scalloped edges.

Miss Blackthorne wanted the musicians to look very feminine. She had the uniforms designed and sewn by the Pettibone Uniform Mfg. in Pittsburgh, Pennsylvania. Not only were they a leading maker of band uniforms, she knew they would work with her to create the proper look. She knew that her detractors would complain that they were just trying to take over positions in men's bands. She thought this was odd as men and women did not play together in the same bands. The band rehearsed together for a year before setting a date for their first concert. At this special event they debuted their new uniforms and the band played Hermann Bellstedt's *Pettibone's Compliment* march as a salute to the company.

Vashti loved this uniform. She knew that the style had been inspired by Helen May Butler, and secretly it was her goal to play in Miss Butler's band and to travel across country seeing this land of opportunity for herself.

This evening as she put on her uniform she dressed with even greater care so that she would look her very best for the performance and for Miss Blackthorne's surprise. Her black high-button shoes were still new and quite stiff. It required a few more minutes with the buttonhook to button them up.

She could hear activity in the other rooms on the second story of their brownstone, indicating that the whole family was making preparations. Father would wear his finest high stand collar with a four-in-hand-tie. His waistcoat would be shown off under a coat with narrow lapels and he was sure to wear his derby. A tuxedo would be dressier, but it also might give away the surprise.

Mother would be wearing her green tulip bell skirt topped by a white blouse with form fitting sleeves and embroidered green leaves on the bodice. Her buttery soft black shoes would show to great effect under the tulip shaped skirt.

Danforth would be dressed "to the nines" so he could impress some of the ladies in the band. He favored cutaway collars and dashing ties, thinking that this drew attention to his handsome cleft chin. He had already begun to call on a few of the ladies. Reginald would look respectable. He was more interested in collecting butterflies and moths, but Mother would see to it that he looked respectable.

Vashti was the first one to the front parlor where they would gather. She didn't sit, but paced around her French horn case and music folder. They would all have to travel to the Founder's Hall on the PRT. Father and Danforth had worked out a scheme to get the cornet into the building with as few people noticing as possible. While the rest of the family went to the hall, Danforth would stop at his favorite billiard hall to watch a game or two until the start of the cakewalk. They knew that Miss Blackthorne would not be backstage at that point and he could enter through the stage door, waiting behind the stage until the moment when he would carry it out into the hall.

In short order the entire family gathered. Their domestic, Hettie McGrew, came to the front door to see them off. As she locked the door behind them she hurried back to the kitchen and out the back door. She put her coat on as she nearly ran down the alleyway and then down the back sidewalks toward the Founder's Hall. She wasn't going to miss this event for all the tea in China!

Other neighbors were walking or riding into town. This was a marvelous annual event and everyone looked forward to it. The conversation was light and merry, the streetcar was packed full, the ladies were seated, gentlemen standing and children were racing between legs and instruments cases. As they got to their stop at Market and N. 2$^{nd}$ Street, it seemed the whole streetcar emptied out.

In the front of the Founder's Hall there were several men from the local constabulary. Sgt. Sean Patrick O'Brien was near to the main entrance. He greeted those he knew by their name and made a point of smiling at other attendees he did not yet know. It was easy duty, but he always wanted a strong police presence when there was a large crowd like tonight's.

Families went to the front entrance, the band members to the side stage door. Some fathers and brothers carried larger instruments, so

Danforth fit right in, but he continued down the alleyway and over to the next street where he walked to Carson Bros. Billiard Hall. He entered through the front door, greeting several friends and rivals as he made his way to the back room. The nicest billiard table was in that room and the best players vied with one another there. It was an unwritten rule that novice players stayed at the front and didn't venture into the hallowed back salon unless they were there to watch an exceptional game.

An exceptional game was in progress. Danforth observed William Casswell and Rodney Starkie playing a game. Casswell had Starkie in a near defeat. One more beautifully executed play and he would win. "Ten ball in the corner pocket." He chalked his cue and bent to sight the ball with the pocket. Gently drawing the cue back, Casswell deftly shot the cue ball into the ten ball and it fell smartly into the pocket and the webbed basket below. Casswell smiled at Starkie and said, "That will cost you a dime, sir."

Starkie pulled out his change purse and paid his debt. Casswell looked around for another worthy opponent. He spotted Danforth. "Come, Danny, you are always ready for a game and a little wager."

Danforth knew that he shouldn't play, because he needed to keep his mind on the time and his delivery.

"Cat got your tongue, Danny? Are you turning coward today? See how the mighty have fallen!" This threat to his character was a little more than Danforth would allow. He felt certain he could finish Casswell off quickly, clear a few cents on a gentleman's wager and still make the cake walk.

"Alright, Casswell. Rack them up!" Danforth carefully placed the cornet against the back wall, took off his coat and prepared to play. It would just be a quick game.

Meanwhile the activity at the Philadelphia Founder's Hall backstage area was frenzied. The general cacophony of instrumentalists warming up created a pleasant din. Everything seemed to be ready. A large blackboard backstage had the order of music written in chalk:

March: *Liberty Bell* - J.P. Sousa
Cornet solo: *The Volunteer*- Walter B. Rogers
March: *Rough Riders* - Geo. Southwell
March: *Philadelphia Patriots* - A. Liberati
Address to the audience with the rules of the cakewalk
Schottische*: Cake Walk* - Geo. Southwell
Thank you
March: *The Stars & Stripes Forever* - J.P. Sousa

Miss Blackthorne walked among the young ladies, complimenting them on their hair or the way their instruments shined. She was, as always, a calming influence. As the clock neared 7 p.m. she began to shoo the band on stage like a mother hen. The band took their seats and the murmur of the crowd grew as their voices filled with civic pride at the spectacle of this ladies' band in their handsome uniforms.

For their part, the ladies were all looking to see where their families were seated. In so doing, they could also see that the grid for the cakewalk was chalked onto the floor in front of the stage. Right at the edge of the stage stood three tables filled with homemade cakes, each cake looking more beautiful and tasty than the next one.

When the band was seated onstage, Amanda Fetkenheuer stood up and the band ceased their warm-up noodling at her signal. In many town bands the solo cornet player was actually the leader. There was no need for a conductor in small bands. Miss Blackthorne had groomed Amanda to be the concertmistress on stage.

The tuba section played a concert B-flat tuning note that all the musicians matched with care as they had been taught. Then they quieted down. Amanda was seated and they waited for Miss Blackthorne to come on to the stage. Pushing aside a curtain, she strode out to the conductor's podium, executed a polite bow and turned to the band. Her uniform was similar to the band's except her skirt was white with blue vertical pin stripes and her jacket was white with gold buttons. She had the flags and bunting on her sleeves as well as navy blue epaulets with braided cords dangling across her chest.

Smiling at the band, she stepped onto the podium and they snapped their instruments onto one knee. When she raised the baton, all instruments came up to the ready position. With a precise preparatory beat the band launched into the march *Liberty Bell* by John Philip Sousa. It was played with spirit and the crowd applauded warmly at the close.

Now it was time for the cornet solo. Amanda stood up next to her chair in the front of the band just to the conductor's right. A flick of the baton brought the opening strains of *The Volunteer* by Walter B. Rogers. After the opening came the cadenza with its plethora of *arpeggios*. Then the polka section ensued with its feats of virtuosity. It was clear that Amanda loved to play the cornet and that the band was well-rehearsed. The slow section at the end caught the audience off guard and the *prestissimo* presentation of *Yankee Doodle* with flourishes served to further excite the crowd. As the last tones sounded Amanda was magnificently applauded. She bowed, acknowledged the band, bowed again and took her seat.

Richard had made his way back stage and was eagerly awaiting Danforth. He should already have been waiting with the cornet in hand. This sent a small shiver of concern across Richard's brain. Danforth wouldn't forget, would he?

Back at the billiard hall Casswell and Danforth were enjoying their game, using every bit of strategy that they could muster. After making a particularly hard bank shot Danforth stood bolt upright. He pulled his pocket watch out of his vest and pushed the button to reveal the face. 7:16! He was late! "Sorry, old chap. We'll have to finish another time. I have to get over to the Founder's Hall or my name will be mud!" Casswell made some noise about being a sore loser, but Danforth pushed his hand through his coat sleeve and said, "Make a diagram of the table. We'll have to continue another time."

Pushing the crowd aside, he found the cornet case, made straight for the front door and took off running down the block, into the alley and to the stage door. Pulling it open, he stepped inside and waited for his eyes to adjust to the dark. Then he saw his father standing with his arms crossed with a look of reproval on his face. "I'm sorry, father. I didn't mean to get involved in a game. Am I still here in enough time?"

"Just barely, my son. I was about to send out the militia," but he was smiling. Richard didn't play billiards as a young man, but he was often caught up in the newest literary work. "The presentation won't happen until after the cakewalk is done. We have time."

"Won't you be missed at the cakewalk?"

"I have Reggie taking my place. Perhaps he'll choose the cake of a young lady who will turn his head away from butterfly catching and the study of larvae. Your mother would be thrilled with that."

In the background, the band was wending its way through the dogfight strain of George Southwell's *Rough Riders* March. Sadie sat dewy-eyed remembering her uncle and occasionally trying to join the band when she was able to moderate her breathing. And then it was done and the crowd applauded wildly.

Mr. Higgins, President of the Benjamin Franklin Free Thinkers Society, stood up and walked to the podium on stage left. He wore a black suit with knee breeches. His stockings were white and led everyone's eyes to his feet where he had those silver buckle shoes that we all associate with Dr. Franklin. The coat was of a modern fashion and he wore a gray sash over his left shoulder, across his chest, and clasped under his right arm at the waist. The sash had tiny blood red piping along the edge. There was also a red fringe at the ends of the sash. The top part of the sash that was over his heart had a black silhouette of the Liberty Bell along with the letters BFFTS emblazoned in black embroidery.

He held up his hand to silence the assembly and in a loud voice intoned, "Ladies and Gentlemen, we are pleased that you were able to join us today for the Ladies Auxiliary to the Benjamin Franklin Free Thinkers Society cakewalk. No doubt you have seen the tasty cakes on display here. I am hoping to bring home this delightfully fluffy coconut cake made by my lovely wife, Mrs. Higgins." He made a grand gesture toward the beautifully ornamented cake.

"Here's how it works, gentlemen. We start out with sixteen people on the square. When Miss Blackthorne starts the band we walk around the square until the music stops. Then the lucky gent who stops on the red square wins a cake. He makes his choice and returns to his seat. Another fellow takes his place until we run out of cakes. We have eighty cakes and have sold eighty tickets to the cakewalk. That also means we have raised eighty dollars for our scholarship fund. Come on down to the front of the hall if you are the lucky holder of one of those tickets. Fill up the squares and we'll have a line off there to the left so that everyone in the hall can see."

The men gathered quickly. They knew the rules of a cakewalk. This annual event had been going on for years. "Step lively, gents, and let's have a little fun! Whenever you are ready, Miss Blackthorne."

Miss Blackthorne stepped to the podium. The horns came to the musicians' knees. She rapped on the podium with her baton for dramatic effect and raised her hands. Everyone snapped into ready position. She gave the band a preparatory beat and they launched into Southwell's *Cake Walk* schottische. The band had to watch closely. Sometimes they played four measures or maybe two measures. Miss Blackthorne would cut them off at random. Whenever they stopped, they would begin again at the very place they had ended. Much hilarity ensued with some of the younger men really strutting to the music. It was the highlight of the evening.

When all the cakes were chosen, the band finished the piece and the crowd responded with enthusiastic applause. Mr. Higgins made his way back to the podium. He was red-faced with excitement. "People, people, people! Thank you for your participation in this evening's event. I want to thank all of the organizers for their hard work. Now we have something else extra special to add to the festivities."

Richard straightened his tie and readied himself to walk to the podium. He and Danforth had rehearsed their roles at home so they were both prepared.

"Please join me in welcoming Prof. Richard Cottingham Smith to the podium to speak for the band members." Richard walked out to polite applause. He was used to lecturing in front of classes, but applause was new for him. He strode out to the front of the stage and the podium. Danforth had worked his way to the other side of the stage to be able to enter behind Miss Blackthorne so she wouldn't see him coming.

"Thank you, Mr. Higgins, ladies and gentlemen. What a splendid job the ladies of the band have done this evening." This brought more applause. "None of this would have been possible without the vision and leadership of Margaret Blackthorne." Miss Blackthorne looked a little uncomfortable at these words, but she accepted them graciously. "I would like to invite Mr. Arthur Ritberger from the C.G. Conn store as well as the special committee from the band to come to the stage." Several men from the audience came forward and stood in a line behind Richard across the stage. "Miss Blackthorne, would you be so kind as to join me here by the podium?" Richard could see past her and saw that Danforth was in his place, still hidden from view with the cornet.

"Miss Blackthorne, you have been such an incredible role model for the women of this community and you have been more generous and philanthropic than any of us will ever know. Just a few months ago your band members decided to honor you for your work." Here he motioned to Danforth, who came forward with the black leather case held out in front of him on his hands. He stopped when he reached the front of the stage right next to Miss Blackthorne. "To that end, we would like to present you with this beautifully engraved Conn Wonder silver cornet." He slowly opened the case to reveal the instrument. Miss Blackthorne was completely caught off guard and held her hands to her cheeks, which were flushed. She was speechless and stood there gazing at the cornet shaking her head from side to side. All the while the assembly had erupted into thunderous applause and had risen to their feet cheering.

The beautifully engraved silver New York Wonder model cornet had been etched at the factory by James H. (Jake) Gardner, C.G. Conn's master engraver.

Richard motioned for the audience to quiet. In a loud voice he read the inscription:

"Lovingly Presented to
Miss Margaret Blackthorne, Directress
Betsy Ross All-Lady Silver Cornet Band
Phila, Penn
July 16, 1899"

Taking the cornet from its purple velvet lined case, she gingerly placed the Benjamin Bent mouthpiece into the receiver and nimbly worked the valves. She smiled. They had been perfectly oiled by someone at the Conn store. This cornet was truly a Wonder.

"Play us a song, Miss Blackthorne," someone called from the band and the whole auditorium resounded with a chorus of un-orchestrated yeses and applause. Miss Blackthorne gently moistened her lips and then the rim of the mouthpiece as her father had taught her to do. She put the cornet to her lips and blew warm air through the horn as if she were fogging a mirror. Then she took a sweet breath and played the pyrotechnic triple tongue finale from John Hartmann's *Home, Sweet Home – Air Varie*. At its close the hall erupted with cheers and the warm applause given to one who is loved.

"Encore! Encore!" came repeated calls.

Miss Blackthorne gave a polite bow of her head and held her hand up to quiet the crowd. She was enjoying putting the cornet through its paces. In a strong voice she announced, "I shall now play for you that touching ballad, *The Last Rose of Summer*."

Again she moistened her lips and then the rim of mouthpiece. The cornet came to her lips. A long, slow breath was taken and a gentle, but well placed articulation commenced the first note of the solo. Miss Blackthorne was a wonderful musician who brought beauty of tone and pathos to the music. At its close you could have heard a pin drop. It seemed that no one could breathe until an audible sniffle came from the back of the band and there was Sadie, dewy-eyed. Then the applause began, built through a crescendo to fortissimo and held for a long time.

Miss Blackthorne gave an elegant bow. She spoke in a full voice to the audience and band members alike. "My dear friends, this is an unexpected gift and honor. To say that I am overwhelmed does not begin to convey the thankfulness that I have in my heart for the wonderful young ladies of this band and their families. I'd like to thank Mr. Smith and the gentlemen of the committee for your thoughtfulness and to you and your wives for entrusting the musical development of your daughters to me. And to Mr. Ritberger of the C.G. Conn store, I am certain that you played no small part in procuring this magnificent instrument." She paused, a little lightheaded. "I am simply humbled and honored. Thank you all from the bottom of my heart." Here she turned to shake hands with Mr. Smith and each of the committee members, ending up with Mr. Ritberger.

When they had left the stage, Mr. Higgins resumed the podium. "That was simply marvelous! And we're not done yet! The band has one more selection to play."

Miss Blackthorne had put the cornet back into the case at the edge of the stage where Danforth had placed it. This way the audience could see it and come up to admire the craftsmanship after the concert. This was one of the things that Danforth and Richard had worked out at home to bring the best effect.

When Miss Blackthorne reached the podium she took up her baton, stepped on to the podium, and the ladies snapped their instruments onto their knees. She raised her baton with great aplomb. The instruments came to the ready position and she gave a crisp preparatory beat to commence John Philip Sousa's *The Stars & Stripes Forever March*.

By the end of the introduction everyone was clapping along to the beat. The hall swelled with patriotic fervor and distinct pride for the Betsy Ross All-Lady Silver Cornet Band. At its close the applause was deafening. Miss Blackthorne motioned for the band to stand

and the applause grew even louder. She bowed several times and then made her way to the floor to greet the crowd.

Many well-wishers came forward to congratulate Miss Blackthorne. They got close up views of the magnificent silver cornet and thanked her profusely. She took time with each and every family, though she felt flushed and a little dizzy. In her mind she just thought it was the excitement of the evening and the crush of the crowd.

The crowd started to move about to socialize with their friends and neighbors. The band began the task of leaving the stage and putting their music and instruments away. Fathers, brothers and beaus came to the stage, gallantly offering to carry instruments for the ladies.

As was her custom when the Great Hall started to empty, she began her rounds after the concert to be certain that all was left in order. It had been a very successful evening for the Ladies Auxiliary to the Benjamin Franklin Freethinker's Society. A significant sum had been raised for their scholarship fund.

For their part, the band members were rewarded with complete surprise from Miss Blackthorne when they had brought out the presentation cornet. It was a miracle that the gift had been kept secret from her. Now as she reflected on the day's performance and the excitement of the presentation cornet she felt a little light-headed and suddenly tired. Her palms were clammy and she felt a little feverish. Well, it was probably the excitement. Plenty of time to rest later at home, but she thought she would play just a few more songs on that cornet to end the day.

She took the cornet out of its case one more time just to experience the sheer joy of corneting. It was both cool and soft to the touch. She loved the way it felt in her hands. Ever since her father had begun to teach her how to blow through the curly tubing, she had reveled in the sound and vibrations that she could feel through her whole body. The ritual moistening of her lips and the mouthpiece was begun. A full, relaxed breath was taken and she launched into the *arpeggio* strain of *Rocked in the Cradle of the Deep*-Grand Fantasia by T.H. Rollinson, crescendoing toward the high C. She stopped short feeling a little strange. Her heart seemed to pound in her chest. Her stomach felt tight and loose all at the same time. She hadn't found those top tones difficult since she first learned to play them. "It's the excitement of the day," she said out loud. "I'll just pack things up and find Stanley. He'll get me home."

In many ways Stanley had become like a father figure to Margaret since her own father had died. Ever patient, he waited elsewhere in the building and then brought the hack to the stage door to convey Miss Blackthorne home. Tonight Stanley went looking for Miss Blackthorne. It seemed to have taken her much longer than usual. He had heard her playing cornet, but the music had stopped abruptly in the middle of a phrase and that was not like her. She didn't go back to fix something and try to perfect the phrase as was her custom. After several minutes he entered the Great Hall where he discovered Miss Blackthorne lying in a heap in front of the stage. Her legs were curled to the right. Though face down, her head was turned to the right and there was a small trickle of blood below her right nostril. Spit was trailing from the corner of her mouth. The cornet had fallen from her left hand and was just inches away from her finger tips, its bell now with a dented rim. He leaned close to her. She wasn't breathing.

Stanley raced out of the hall, out of the building and down the gas lit street three blocks to the police station. He burst into the front door and, gasping for breath, shouted, "Someone has to come right now! Miss Blackthorne is dead!"

This caught the attention of Sgt. Sean O'Brien, who walked briskly to the front of the station house and spoke to Stanley in his gentle voice, "Calm down, Stanley. What's this business about Miss Blackthorne being dead? I was there for the concert and she was doing just fine."

Having caught his breath, Stanley could give more of an account to Sgt. O'Brien. "I heard Miss Blackthorne practicing in the Great Hall. She stopped right before she hit the high note, but she didn't go back to fix it. It was quiet for several minutes. I knew something was wrong and when I went into the Great Hall, I discovered her. You've got to come!"

Sean O'Brien grabbed his hat and ran through the swinging doors that marked the border between public space and policeman's domain. He was out the front door at full stride with Stanley running close behind him. In the old country, Sean Patrick O'Brien was known for having a lip for the cornet. He had been a front row man in the St. Bilfrid Brass Band. He knew Miss Blackthorne and he knew something was wrong. Sergeant O'Brien and Stanley rushed into the hall and up to the stage. There lay Miss Blackthorne.

"Did you touch her, Stanley?"

"No, sir, Sergeant."

"This is exactly how you found her?"

"No, sir, it isn't."

The hair on the back of O'Brien's neck stood on end. "What's different Stanley?"

"You see that long stemmed red rose near the top of her head?"

"Yes."

"That wasn't there when I left."

# Chapter 4

One of the regular beat cops had seen Sgt. O'Brien and Stanley running toward the Founder's Hall. He followed them, hoping he could help. As Sgt. O'Brien and Stanley stood in the hall staring at Miss Blackthorne, Patrolman Brinkman ran up between them. "Oh, my!" he exclaimed as he stopped still in his tracks like a *cesura* in a Rossini Overture. For a grand pause moment no one said a thing, then O'Brien crossed himself and started barking orders at Brinkman.

"Get back to the station. Order the coroner to come here immediately. Have the man who does the pictures brought here with his camera. We'll need patrolmen outside of the hall to keep people away. If there's any evidence here I want it found. Stanley, you come with me. There's no need for you to look at this ghastly scene."

Brinkman ran down the street, his tall policeman's cap bouncing, and he gripped his nightstick in his right hand. Bursting into the station, he hollered, "Boys, we got us a murder to solve!" This caught everyone's attention. This was real police work, not just saving some dowager's cat from a tree or making sure the young boys were staying away from the peep shows on the seedier side of town. Several patrolmen hurried to the Founder's Hall where Sgt. O'Brien posted them around the perimeter.

Dr. Mortimer "Morty" Harrison the coroner arrived and pronounced Margaret Blackthorne dead. He waited for the photographer before moving the body. He thought he saw something around Miss Blackthorne's mouth. He couldn't be certain what this was until he got her back to the morgue. There he could run some tests.

Morty wondered where the guy with the cameras was. At this rate *rigor mortis* would be setting in and it would be difficult to lay the body flat on the stretcher. Morty knew that the photographs helped the policemen in their investigations, but he was a medical science man, a chemist. He detested waiting for someone to haul those big contraptions with their glass plates and flashers. The police department had begun to employ William “Flash” Manily for photographs. Flash was a young buck in his late twenties. He was a strapping fella who could carry his ungainly equipment into unusual spaces where crimes seemed to always be committed. Best of all, he was very professional about his work and would not make extra photographs to sell to the local newspapers.

In due time Manily appeared. One of the police paddy wagons had been sent to his house to pick him and his equipment up. Some of the officers helped to carry the heavy equipment into the hall.

“Easy, gents. Set it down carefully, not like you’re bouncing a babe on your knee. Those glass plates can break easy enough.” Flash looked over at coroner Harrison. “There’s a pack of reporters out there prowling around like wolves looking for a story.”

“Did you give ‘em one?”

“No sir, Dr. Harrison. I know better than that. I just thought someone ought to know.”

“You get to work and I’ll relay that information to O’Brien. He was the first on the scene.”

One of the officers in the paddy wagon had told Flash that the deceased was Margaret Blackthorne, but he was always shocked by what he had to photograph at crime scenes. He was glad to be helping out the police and it was good to have the extra monies paid to his fledgling business, but he wasn’t sure that he could keep this up for much longer. Fortunately, this crime scene wasn’t gruesome. He wondered why they thought this was a murder. Maybe she just fell over dead. Eventually it happens to us all. Miss Blackthorne seemed a little young for that, but from what he had heard, the woman was a hard worker from way back. She worked more than she slept. He was cogitating these things as he set up his camera.

Morty Harrison walked to the back of the hall where O’Brien was gently interrogating Stanley Robinson. “You sure you don’t know anyone who made any threats toward Miss Blackthorne? Maybe she got a note under her door or something."

"No, sir. I know there were people who didn't like Miss Blackthorne for being a successful business lady. I know there were some who didn't like her starting the ladies band, but I never knew of any threats made right towards her. She was always such a sweet, kind lady. I just don't know of anyone who would do such a terrible thing." Stanley's cheeks were tear stained and he was staring unseeingly into space.

Morty motioned for O'Brien to come over to him. O'Brien patted Stanley's shoulder, stood up and walked over by Morty. "Sergeant, I thought that you would like to know that the perimeter is crawling with reporters. Flash saw them when he came in."

"We won't be able to keep this out of the newspapers forever. Stanley doesn't seem to know anything. I'll send him home and then you and I will look over the crime scene."

Walking back toward Stanley, O'Brien mustered a caring smile for Stanley and said, "You can go home now. If there are any more questions, we'll know where to find you. Stanley, I'm sorry for your loss."

Stanley rose on wobbly legs, straightened his back and walked heavily toward the stage door.

"Stanley?"

He spun quickly toward O'Brien.

"Was there ever a guard at that stage door?"

"No, sir."

"Who opens and closes the building?"

"Fella named Forbes. He's usually in the boiler room. He reads the comic strips down there."

"Thank you, Stanley. Go home and try to get some rest."

O'Brien watched as Stanley walked out of the building. He could understand a little about Stanley Robinson's grief. To be sure, it was for an employer who had treated him well, but he was probably wondering about his future and where he would find another job. He was an old man and a negro. It was a rare person like Margaret Blackthorne who treated everyone with respect and dignity. As the son of immigrant Irish parents, Sean O'Brien had felt the sharp tongue of discrimination regarding the shanty Irish. He determined at a young age to prove his worth and find a *niche* in his new homeland. For him, this had proven to be police work. He really didn't know what Stanley was going to do. The road was much harder for a negro, but Stanley had risen through the ranks at Blackthorne Bunting Works. Maybe they would keep him on, or perhaps he could work his way up all over again.

♫

Flash was taking his last photograph. The air smelled like sulfur from the flash. One last poof and he'd have all the angles covered.

"Anything else you can think of, Dr. Harrison?"

"No, Flash. That will be it, unless Sgt. O'Brien has other ideas."

O'Brien had walked up on the end of the conversation. "I think that's fine, Flash. Get those photographs developed as fast as you can and get them to me tomorrow. I'll let the Chief know that they are coming."

Morty motioned for two of the policemen to help move Miss Blackthorne's body. He would roll her over and try to straighten out her legs if he could. Then they would lift her on to a stretcher, cover her up with a green wool blanket and carry her out to the coroner's hearse. He and his driver would take her to the morgue and he would start his investigation. He knew he'd be at this all night.

With a prominent citizen like Margaret Blackthorne, the Chief and the populace would want answers quickly.

O'Brien watched as Flash packed things up and got two more policemen to help him carry his equipment back out to the paddy wagon. He would also have a long night at his photographer's studio.

Coroner Harrison was ready to leave as well. Sgt. O'Brien walked out in front of both men and their minions, calling out "Alright, pressmen! If you will gather around me, I'll give you as much of the story as I am able. Sometime after the Ladies Auxiliary to the Benjamin Franklin Freethinker's Society cakewalk, Miss Margaret Blackthorne was found dead by her driver, Stanley Robinson. We do not know the cause of death."

"Was she murdered?"

"We don't know yet."

"Can you speculate, Sergeant?"

"Now boys, I've told you all I know. We won't know much more for several days. Someone will let you know when we know anything more. You might as well go back to your newsrooms. There's nothing more here."

The crowd slouched away, putting their pencils and pads in various pockets. O'Brien was a stickler for department rules, but he was a straight-up fella and was always fair to the men of the press. They would just have to play the waiting game. The sweaty pressroom, card games and coffee that tasted like mud were in their immediate futures.

O'Brien walked back into the hall. Young Brinkman was waiting there. O'Brien liked Brinkman. He was the same age as his son Jack, played the alto horn, was as smart as a whip, but knew when to keep his mouth shut.

"Brinkman, find the caretaker. His name is Forbes. Try the boiler room. Bring him back here."

Turning toward the other policemen, he ordered, "the rest of you will return to walking your beats as the doors are locked. Keep a watchful eye out, boys. We may have a killer on the loose."

Behind the stage was an iron spiral staircase leading down to the bowels of the Philadelphia Founders Hall. Brinkman spiraled down the stairs and stopped cold. There was very little light and he had to let his eyes adjust. When he could see, he grabbed his nightstick from its leather loop on his belt and crept slowly down the dank hallway. There was still a killer on the loose and this would be an ideal place to hide.

About fifteen feet down the hallway was a sliver of light peeking out from the boiler room. Brinkman snuck forward to get a look into the room. Being summer, there was no need for the boilers, so all was quiet. He could see a plain wood desk with a newspaper folded to the comic strip page.

A couple more steps revealed feet on the corner of the desk, followed by long legs, a body and a scruffy bearded man with wire rimmed glasses pushed up on his forehead. Brinkman stopped for a moment. He could see the man's chest rising and falling in peaceful sleep. He took his nightstick and gently rapped on the steel door. The man snorted awake, grabbed his glasses and looked around.

"You Forbes?"

"Hmm, yup." He wasn't quite awake yet.

"Sgt. O'Brien wants you upstairs to lock the hall."

Forbes was awake now. He realized that he was talking to a policeman. "Is there a problem?"

"Yes, there is. Sgt. O'Brien will speak with you. I'm just to bring you to him. Be sure you bring your keys."

Forbes' eyes were wide open now and the two men raced up the curly iron staircase and out to the front of the stage.

"You Forbes?"

"Yes, sir, Phineas Forbes."

Brinkman took out his beat notebook and wrote this down.

"Where have you been this evening?"

"In the boiler room, sir. I come down in the afternoon to open the stage door and put the lights on backstage. About an hour and a half before the cakewalk this evening I set the tables up for the cakes, then I opened the entryway doors and put the rest of the lights in the hall on. Not much else for me to do. These folks run the show themselves."

"Mr. Forbes, we have had a death here this evening. It might be a murder."

Forbes' eyes bugged out.

"Miss Blackthorne was found dead after the concert and the cakewalk. Where were you?"

Falling over his tongue, Forbes tried to answer, but the words were just a jumble.

"Calm down, Mr. Forbes. I just want to find out where you were."

Forbes gulped and managed to sputter "In the boiler room. I'm always in the boiler room."

"Alright, Mr. Forbes. Just take a look at this space. Does anything look out of place to you? Do you see anything unusual?"

Forbes began to look around. O'Brien watched him with a practiced eye. Forbes wasn't the killer. He had been startled by the news about Miss Blackthorne, and he seemed to be on the up-and-up.

Walking on the stage, Forbes counted the chairs. With O'Brien and Brinkman following, he walked back stage.

"This is different." He said pointing toward a table. "This table put here to hold the presentation cornet for Miss Blackthorne, but I set it up at the first curtain leg. Not here in the back. I don't know that it is important, but you asked what was different."

"Keep looking, Mr. Forbes.

"I will, sir. Miss Blackthorne was a marvelous person. I just can't imagine." His voice trailed off as he looked down at his feet and gave a deep sigh.

Sean put his hand on Forbes' shoulder, "Patrolman Brinkman will write down anything out of place. Then please go around the outside of the hall and lock up as you go. I would like to get my men back out on the street."

So Forbes, O'Brien and Brinkman made the rounds and found nothing else out of place. Brinkman took down Phineas Forbes's address and O'Brien said they would be in touch if they had more questions. "You can lock up the rest of the hall and go home. Be careful not to talk about anything that has happened at the hall tonight."

In the alley outside the stage door, O'Brien and Brinkman stood for a moment.

"Well, Brinkman, that's about all we can do here. Let's head back to the station. There's plenty of paperwork to be done. The coroner's report and photographs won't be ready for some time."

"Sgt. O'Brien, I would like to do the paperwork for this case. I've never been involved in a murder investigation before and I hope to be an inspector one day."

"Son, we don't know that it is a murder yet, so be careful how you talk about it."

"Yes sir. I will."

O'Brien and Brinkman walked back to the station. Things had calmed down for the moment. O'Brien would call "The Roundhouse," the name for police headquarters. He'd leave a report of what he knew thus far. It was good that Brinkman wanted to do the paperwork. Sean O'Brien had never learned to spell very well, but he was always able to draft someone to take care of that onerous task. His strength was in talking people out of jumping off buildings and calming down drunks.

# Chapter 5

Morty walked into the coroner's office and held the door open for the two men carrying the stretcher. Another patrolman carried the cornet in its shiny black case and the rose lying on top.

"Set the cornet case on the counter and Miss Blackthorne on the table there, men. Thanks for your help."

"Anything else you need, Doc?"

"No. You men check in with your precincts and go back on duty."

The three men left Harrison's office, closing the door on their way out. He got to work right away. This was sure to be a high level case and he didn't want the chief breathing down his neck. The sooner he got to work, the more information he would have come morning.

He already suspected the cause of death. At the Great Hall he had noticed a telltale ring of yellow on her lips. If his suspicion was right, this was a murder.

Yellow rings could indicate the presence of arsenic. He would need to test for trace elements and he'd start with the skin around her lips. He had enough equipment here to find the answer to what had killed her. Then it would be up to the police to find her murderer.

Walking over to the table, Harrison took a small sample of tissue from Miss Blackthorne's lips and placed it on a glass slide. The glass slide was then placed into a test tube. If it was arsenic, a silvery-black residue would be produced inside the tube when held in a flame. He set to work with his first test. He needed to be both careful and efficient. The body would decompose rapidly in the heat of summer. If the test proved positive, he would know the cause of death. Then he would just need to figure out how the arsenic had been administered.

Within a few minutes he had his answer. A silvery-black deposit appeared. This was arsenic poisoning all right. He went over to the cornet to look for evidence of arsenic on it. He swabbed the mouthpiece, placed the swab in another test tube and performed the same test. There was that same telltale silvery-black residue.

Harrison was now convinced that this was a murder, but who was the killer? The question would fall back into the hands of the police. All he could do now was write up his report and release the body to the funeral parlor when the police chief approved his findings. In the meantime he could put Miss Blackthorne's body into one of the refrigerated holds. The ice would slow the body's decomposition.

He looked at the large black and white clock to see what time it was. Eleven fifty-six p.m. He would need to have the telephone operator make calls for him upstairs. Maybe he could find some coffee. With the paperwork to be done it would be a couple more hours before he could go home and get some shut-eye. He'd need it. Tomorrow would be a busy day.

# Chapter 6

"Extra! Extra! Read all about it! Miss Margaret Blackthorne found dead." The newspaper boys were out early hawking the morning edition of the Philadelphia Tribune and they were doing a brisk business. It was a complete shock to the whole city of Philadelphia. Last night Miss Blackthorne was a local heroine. The night editor had already sent the morning edition to press when he had to stop the evening presses for the "extra." What had been a glowing tribute now expanded to an homage to the dear woman.

Richard Smith had heard the excitement and had gone out to get the "extra". He returned to the house with downcast eyes reading the front page. His wife was sitting in the front parlor of their brownstone home watching him carefully. The pucker of his forehead told her that all was not well. When he looked up from the newspaper and in her direction she raised her eyebrows to show her concern and wait for his reply.

"It's a tragedy, Elisabeth," he said with a soft voice and heavy heart. "Miss Blackthorne is dead."

"Good heavens, Richard! Does it say how she died?"

He kept his voice low so that Vashti would not hear the conversation. He would prefer to tell his daughter to her face. Vashti was a sensible girl. She had a good head on her shoulders and wasn't given to day-dreaming or vapors, but she loved Miss Blackthorne. So did all of the ladies in the band. At least this was always what he had thought. "The paper hints that it may have been murder. They have been careful in their use of syntax. My dear, who would want to murder a lovely, civic-minded person like Margaret Blackthorne? Think of all she has done for the community and especially for our daughter."

"I don't know what to say, Richard. I'm as shocked as you. I know there were those who didn't agree with her teaching ladies to be responsible through her band work, but to murder someone over music? It doesn't seem possible. Maybe it was an accident."

"Dearest one, our first concern will be to break this horrid news to our petite Vashti." This had been a pet name for his daughter since she was a tiny, tiny baby. He still used it with her when he wanted to show his deep love for her without being overly demonstrative.

"Well, Richard, we'll tell her together as soon as she comes downstairs. Our Vashti is a strong, young lady. We have raised her to use her thoughts and not to let her emotions get the best of her."

Richard nodded his agreement. "I am concerned about some of the other young ladies in the band. That band has been a tremendous influence in their lives. I wonder if anyone would be able to fill Miss Blackthorne's place?"

They both heard the sound of little feet skipping down the carpeted stairs. Vashti burst into the room like a *fortepiano* in a Verdi Opera. One look at her parents and she knew that something terrible had happened. Her father's brow was puckered. Her mother sat primly by her table with her favorite rose print cup of tea that had long since cooled off. She sat with her hands firmly clasped. This was a sure sign of something amiss. Stopping in her tracks she asked, "What's wrong? I can see concern written all over your faces."

"Come and sit by me, Vashti. Your father and I have some very sad news to tell you." Vashti crossed the room to the rose settee, seated herself and performed the identical raised eyebrow motion as her mother. She waited.

"My sweet, petite Vashti, someone you love is no longer of this earth. Miss Blackthorne has died." Elisabeth put her arms around her daughter's shoulders. Vashti was holding her breath, trying to make sense of this news. When she finally exhaled she gasped, "How do you know?" Richard showed her the front page of the "extra". Over a photo of Miss Blackthorne in her band uniform was the headline:

MARGARET BLACKTHORNE – MURDERED?

She re-read the headline a few times just to let the news sink in and to steady herself. "I heard the newsboys shouting down the street, but I just thought it was something financial." After a pause, "How did she die?"

"I've just read the first two paragraphs," said her father. "If the reporter has followed newspaper style, there isn't any information to indicate how she died. It just says that she was found by her driver, Stanley Robertson, who ran from the Great Hall to the police station. He brought Sgt. O'Brien back to the crime scene with him. There aren't any more pertinent facts. The writer then switches to a quote from Sgt. O'Brien about heading the investigation followed by a narrative of Miss Blackthorne's work in the community."

Vashti's eyes were welling up with tears. Her beloved band director dead? How could this be? Vashti didn't hear much of her father's recitation on literary style. She heard that Jack O'Brien's father was leading the investigation and she knew that another the trip to the C.G. Conn store was now more important than just a piccolo that wouldn't peep. She had to talk to Jack.

Taking her hankie from her pocket she dabbed her eyes and daintily blew her nose. "I can't imagine how the band members are taking this news! What will happen to the band? Will we play for Miss Blackthorne's funeral? There's so much that is unsettled." She paused to ponder her next move fully aware that her parents were watching her. "Mother, may I go visit with Christina and Sadie? It think it would be beneficial for us to be together at a time of loss such as this."

Elisabeth Smith knew her daughter too well to think that her only goal was to help comfort friends. Vashti wasn't afraid to be in the band or to try new things. Under her slightly unruly brown curls was a very good mind and Elisabeth reveled in her daughter's strength. "I think that it will be wonderful for you to go to your friends at a sad time like this. It will certainly be of great comfort to them all."

# Chapter 7

It was 6 a.m. and Sean O'Brien was rubbing sleep out of his eyes on the way to the kitchen. Last evening's sleep was only four hours. He'd be working long hours for the next couple of days.

"You're a sight for sore eyes, Sean Patrick," whispered Molly. There by the black cast iron stove stood his wife of 24 years. She was smiling at him and had bacon frying in a skillet. "And how many eggs would himself like this morning?"

"Three, my good wife."

They were both born in Philadelphia, but their parents had immigrated to the United States during the Great Famine in Ireland. Molly and Sean had six children - Jack, Erin, Rachel, George, Ian and Mary. They had a good life in the new world and the two of them were building a better life for their children.

Molly brought him a cup of steaming hot black coffee and cracked three eggs into a second skillet. She put four slices of freshly made bread on the stove's toaster racks near the stove pipe.

"I expect we'll know a great deal more about Miss Blackthorne's death today. I just can't imagine who would want to kill a nice lady like her."

"Do you think it's a murder, Sean?"

"I have a bad feeling about this, Molly. I think she was too young to have fallen over dead from a heart attack, but it just doesn't feel right."

Molly flipped the eggs one at a time and deftly turned the toast pieces so they would not burn. She pulled out four strips of bacon and put them on Sean's plate. This was an unusually generous amount of bacon, but she knew that he might not be able to eat lunch today even if she sent a meal over to the station. The toast was retrieved and buttered. Three perfectly fried, over-easy eggs went onto the plate and she carried it to the table and set it before her husband. Sean picked up his fork and was just about to snag a piece of bacon when Molly cleared her throat. Sean looked up at here wondering what he had done.

“Haven’t you forgotten something, Mr. O’Brien?”

“Of course, my dear.”

They both bowed their heads and said grace.

“I’ll try to send lunch to you, Sean, even though I know you’ll be working a long day today. You just tend to your work. We’ll be all right here at home.”

“Thank you Molly. I appreciate that.”

He ate in silence while Molly tidied up the kitchen in preparation for when the children would get up. Jack would be first. He was the oldest and had his work to do, too. When Sean had come home the night before, Jack was still awake. He had been at the concert and was shocked to hear the news about Miss Blackthorne’s death. Sean was careful not to talk about the case. He was always careful, but if this was a murder, the story would spread through the band musician world faster than a circus band playing a gallop.

Molly broke into his thoughts. “Here are your boots, Sgt. O’Brien. Jack put your boots out in the hall with his shoes last night. He thought you might be talking to the press today and should look your best.”

Sean smiled at Molly, who was bursting with a mother’s pride. They were so thrilled at the way their oldest son was growing up. He was working in a good business establishment. He was interested in dancing and was showing interest in some of the fine young women in the band. He must surely find a good woman who would understand his passion for fixing musical instruments, but his thoughtfulness showed that he was growing into a fine young man and they were pleased.

As Sean slipped his second boot on and began to lace it up, Jack tiptoed out of the room he shared with his brothers.

“Thank you for having my boots polished, Jack. That was very thoughtful of you, son.”

“You’re welcome, Pop. I thought you might be talking to a lot of reporters today. Shoes that shine make a great impression.”

“You make your mother and me proud, son.”

Jack smiled and shrugged. “Will you be able to talk about this more this evening? I know that all of the musicians will be talking about it at the store today. Anyone who is as prominent as Miss Blackthorne will certainly get a lot of press. Those band girls are going to miss her!”

“I am waiting to hear from the coroner as to what the cause of death might be. If there’s anything amiss, we’ll have to investigate further. Until that point, she’s just an unfortunate who happens to have fallen over dead. May God rest her soul.” Slipping his coat on, he kissed Molly, put his hand on Jack’s shoulder and headed out the door.

“How would you like your eggs this morning, my son?”

“Over hard, please.”

She slipped two eggs into the pan. Now that Jack was a workingman she gave him extra bacon and two eggs to make it through his day. He liked to grab a quick sandwich with Daniel O’Toole for dinner. Daniel was a widower and he didn’t pack a meal for himself. There was a nice little Horn & Hardart about two blocks from Conn where the two went for their lunch. They could talk shop together.

Jack loved the Horn & Hardart. He could get anything he wanted by opening the little glass door and taking out a sandwich, a piece of apple pie or even chocolate pudding. It wasn't exactly mechanical, but, when he opened his chosen glass door, he could see enough of what went on behind the wall of doors to appreciate the process that had been invented. Daniel had even gotten him to try the coffee. Horn & Hardart cafeterias were known for their New Orleans-style coffee. Coffee beans were blended with chicory. It was an interesting taste that he wasn't exactly wild about, but it made him feel a little cultured to drink it. Daniel said it would grow on him.

Secretly, Jack was trying to invent a system that would replace the workers behind the wall of doors. He had a couple of mechanical theories that had the food traveling along on a system of rollers, but he didn't know how to get it off of the rollers and into the cubbie holes. As yet, these theories were only mind musings and not a working concept.

"Anything special happening at the Conn store today?"

"I think it will all be routine today, except for the news on Miss Blackthorne. If it has made it into the morning edition, people will probably stop in the store to talk about it. Conn has always been a place for musicians to gather to talk about last night's concert or which new trombone player is now with Sousa and His Band. It's one of the things that I like about working there. It's the heart of music for many people around the country. The players from the touring bands stop in there all the time."

"Well, my son, I am glad that you enjoy your work and that you get to learn from Mr. O'Toole. He's a good man."

♫

Sean was walking toward the station. He enjoyed walking in the early morning. The streets were still quiet, except for the merchants who were getting ready to open their stores. Back in the days when he walked a beat, he enjoyed taking the time to talk to people and get to know them. It was, to his mind, the best way to do police work. You had to know the people and their families. If you caught a youngster doing something minor, you could take him home and his parents would sort things out.

He could see that the newsboys were already on their routes. It was likely that the whole city would know about Miss Blackthorne's death by nine a.m. The morning edition would take care of that.

"Morning, Evans. Hear anything from the coroner yet?"

"Yes, Sergeant. There is a report on your desk and good morning to you, too, sir."

He walked into his office, took off the blue coat and his hat, hung them on a coat tree near the door and sat down in his wooden chair. It squeaked as he rolled toward the desk. This was the part of his job that he hated. It was bad enough to find a body, but then the report would come through and he would have to read through it with all the gruesome details.

He sighed as he picked up the coroner's folder. "Why Miss Blackthorne?" he spoke out loud. He undid the string that secured the top flap. He pulled out the report written in Dr. Morty Harrison's beautiful script. Fortunately this report was far less gruesome than some, but there it was in black ink. Cause of death: arsenic poisoning. He walked out of his office and up to Evans's desk. "Get me the Chief of Police on the telephone, Evans. Switch it into my office when you have him on the line."

He walked back into the office to wait, but it wasn't long before the black telephone on his desk rang. He picked it up, held the earpiece to his right ear and spoke into the mouthpiece. "O'Brien, here."

"O'Brien, this is Chief Miller. What's the news on the Blackthorne case?"

"It's arsenic poisoning, sir. Looks like she was murdered."

"Phew! I didn't expect that. It's such a shame. Nice lady like that, who could possibly want to kill her? Well, I'll have my office get a statement out to the press. You get started on the investigation. Anything you need is at your disposal."

"Thank you, Chief. We'll find the culprit."

He hung up the phone and walked to the outer office. He knew Evans had been listening on the line. "Get Brinkman here as soon as possible."

"Yes, sir. Going to be a long day."

"Several long days until we get the killer."

Back in his office he began to formulate questions and a list of suspects. The coroner's report said the arsenic was found on the mouthpiece of the cornet, so someone had to have put it there, but how? Who had access to that instrument? Was it someone at Conn? How did that person get the arsenic in the first place? Was it someone else? Where was the cornet after it left the store? Could there have been someone else who had access to the instrument?

Brinkman came into the office and waited for instructions. O'Brien looked up and said, "It's a murder, Brinkman."

"Wow! This is my first murder investigation, Sergeant!"

"Calm down, Brinkman. It's a very long process. Hope you brought your notepad. We'll talk to a lot of people today. I will want you to write down each question and the answers that are given by each person to whom we talk. There's a wagon out front. They'll take us to the Conn store. That's the logical place to start."

Grabbing his coat and hat he headed for the street with Brinkman right behind as they paraded out the front door. He was glad that Molly had the presence of mind to cook him a large breakfast. She was a good woman, but so was Margaret Blackthorne. Whatever could be the motive for killing her?

# Chapter 8

"Remember, Brinkman, I ask the questions. If you think of something I've missed we'll discuss it later. Understood? We can always go back for more information."

"Yes, sir." Brinkman respected Sean O'Brien and he knew better than to try and upstage him. He had known O'Brien for most of his life and he actually had been inspired to pursue police work because of Sean O'Brien. He was also pretty sure that O'Brien was willing to teach him police business, otherwise he wouldn't be along on this case.

Climbing out of the wagon O'Brien and Brinkman walked across the sidewalk and revolved their way into the Conn store. It had only been open a short time, but there were already people in the store shopping. O'Brien spied Mr. Ritberger up in the window of his second story office. Ritberger caught his eye and motioned that he was on his way down. In less than thirty seconds he greeted O'Brien. All of the musicians in town knew Arthur Ritberger. Many had purchased instruments and supplies like valve oil from his store. Sean had brought his cornet in to be serviced over the years. "How may I be of help to you today?"

"I'm Sergeant O'Brien"

Ritberger interrupted. "You play the cornet."

"Yes, I do." He smiled.

"And you are Jack's father. Yes?" Ritberger had a good memory.

"That's correct. This is Patrolman Brinkman. May we speak in your office?"

Mr. Ritberger reached out to shake Brinkman's hand. "Certainly. Follow me."

Sean cast a glance around the store. Following Ritberger, they all walked down the hallway and up the three steps. O'Brien took note of the beautifully appointed office and thought that there must be quite a lot of money in band instruments these days. "Please, have a seat." Ritberger said, pulling the door closed behind him.

"Thanks, we'll stand. Mr. Ritberger, perhaps you are aware that Margaret Blackthorne was found dead last night."

"I read it in the extra edition of the newspaper this morning. It was quite a shock. I was at the cakewalk and concert last night. We provided the elegant presentation cornet that the band gave to Miss Blackthorne."

"Can you tell me who had access to the cornet?"

"A number of people. Why do you ask?"

"Because we believe that Miss Blackthorne may have been murdered and it has something to do with that cornet. We'd like to question those who came into contact with the instrument."

Ritberger suddenly felt dizzy. He sat down at his desk. "Sergeant, are you suggesting that we have a murderer at C.G. Conn?"

"I'm just asking questions, Mr. Ritberger. Who had access to that cornet?"

Ritberger shook his head in disbelief. Surely no one at his store would want to kill Miss Blackthorne.

"Please, Mr. Ritberger, who had access to that cornet?"

He snapped out of his daze. "I'm sorry, Sergeant, I was just trying to take this all in. Miss Blackthorne was a good friend."

"I'm sorry for your loss, but it would be a help to have a list of people who had access to that cornet."

Ritberger shook his head as if to clear it. “Now, you were asking for a list of people who came into contact with the cornet. Let me see, myself, Bruno Stein, our brass craftsman, Daniel O’Toole, our master craftsman and his apprentice, Jack O’Brien.”

O’Brien held his breath for one long moment. He hadn’t expected to find his son on a list of murder suspects. “Can you tell me anyone who would have wanted her dead?”

“She was such a boon to our business that I can’t imagine anyone here would have wanted her dead.” He looked very distraught.

“These are just routine questions Mr. Ritberger. We have just begun our investigation.”

“I know that there are a number of bandsmen who are not happy that she started a ladies band. They are afraid that she’ll be taking away their job. I guess that won’t happen now.”

“Got any names for us?”

“It’s just the talk that I hear in the store. I don’t actually play in a band anymore. There just isn’t enough time to keep up my lip. I’m a flute player.”

“Could we use your office to question these three men?”

“Certainly.” He stood up. “Who would you like first? I’ll bring him up here myself.”

“Mr. Stein, I think. Please, don’t tell him or anyone else why we are here.”

Stein entered the office. He was a man of about 60 years of age. His once dark hair was streaked with silver, as was his bushy moustache. He wore wire rimmed glasses and his clothing, while appropriate for a craftsman, was clean with crisply ironed shirt and trousers.

"I am Bruno Stein. Mr. Ritberger says you want to talk with me." He met O'Brien's eyes easily and with a glint of questioning.

"Yes, Mr. Stein. I am Sgt. O'Brien and this is Patrolman Brinkman. Please, have a seat."

Stein strode forward and pulled out one of the mahogany chairs with the detailed leather seat and settled himself. "Did you work on the presentation cornet that was given last night to Margaret Blackthorne when it came to this store?"

"I did. I take care of all the brass instruments that come into the store."

"What do you do when a new instrument comes in?"

"I check all of the slides to see that they are properly fitted and that they are lubricated. Then I check the valves to be certain they seat properly and there is no friction with the valve casing. If that all checks out, I play test the instrument by running through some scales to see if the instrument leaks."

"Is this what you did with the Blackthorne cornet?"

"Yes, sir. A special presentation cornet like that is given even more attention at the factory, but I checked it over just like I would every brass instrument that comes in here. At the end I wiped the cornet clean of any fingerprints and put it back in the case."

"Did you wipe the mouthpiece off?"

"No need to. I use my own mouthpiece kept on my bench in the back."

"Where did that cornet go when you were done with it?"

"I carried it over to Daniel O'Toole. He checks over all the work before anything goes out to the customer."

"Did you notice anything usual about this band instrument?"

“Aside from the beautiful engraving, no sir.”

“Did you know Miss Blackthorne?”

“Just by sight. I never met her.”

“Thank you, Mr. Stein. Please, do not share this conversation with anyone, not even your wife. You may go back to your work.”

Stein stood up and walked out of the office. Ritberger had been waiting in the hallway and stepped inside the office. “May I bring the next person in?”

“Yes. Please bring in Daniel O’Toole.”

Sean had known Daniel for years. He didn’t like having to question a family friend, but soon he’d be questioning his own son. He looked to Brinkman who was finishing notes on his pad.

“Did you notice anything unusual, Brinkman?”

“No, sir. He was forthcoming with information and doesn’t seem to have a motive.”

The etched glass door opened and in walked Daniel O’Toole. “Hello, Sean.” He greeted him with a warm smile and reached out to shake hands.

Sean shook Daniel’s hand. “Hello, Daniel. I’m afraid that I am here in an official capacity today. We’ll dispense with the niceties.”

“I take it, Sgt. O’Brien, that this has something to do with the death of Margaret Blackthorne.”

“Maybe, Mr. O’Toole. How about letting me ask the questions?” Sean smiled and gestured for Daniel to have a seat. He went through the same questions that he had asked Stein. “Can you think of anyone who would want to kill Miss Blackthorne?”

"I can't imagine anyone here would have a reason. All those girls bought their band instruments right here. That girl band has been great for business!"

"Ritberger mentioned that some of the men's bands didn't like her starting an all-lady band. What do you think? Could some fella have a beef with her?"

"I think some people are always looking for something to find fault in. Likely some of those bandsmen don't want to see women out and about. Miss Blackthorne created an outstanding, artistic band in three or four years and she did it with young girls. It might have embarrassed 'em to see what she could do. Showed 'em up, don't 'cha know."

"Any names for me?"

"I think you ought to check out some of the blokes in the Pick-Penn Company Band. There's at least one fella in there who's kinda vocal about Miss Blackthorne. Name's Casswell."

"One more question, Daniel, and you must not share this with anyone." Daniel nodded. "Is there any arsenic used here in the store?"

Daniel's eyes widened. "There's no arsenic used here."

"Thank you, Daniel. Keep this quiet. Do not talk to anyone here about this. You may go back to work. Contact me if you think of anything else. Keep it professional, not at our Sunday dinners. Understand?" Daniel nodded, rose slowly and straightened the leather apron that he always wore at work and walked out of the office. He was stooped over from all his years of working at his woodwind bench, but he was still a very vital man. Sean didn't like having to question him, but he was sure that Daniel had given him a good lead. Ritberger knocked on the door and, when Sean replied, he opened the door and asked if they were ready for the next person.

"Yes, Mr. Ritberger. Send Jack in." In a few minutes the etched door opened and Jack bounded up the steps. "Wow! Would you look at this place! I've only peeked in through the door."

"Settled down, Jack. Have a seat."

"Okay, Pop."

"That would be "yes, sir." We'll keep this in an official capacity."

"Yes, sir. Why are you here?"

"We are investigating the death of Margaret Blackthorne."

"Whoa!"

"Now, if you don't mind, I'll ask the questions," he said kindly, while shaking his head slightly at his son's reaction.

"Brinkman, be very thorough about writing things down exactly. Note that Jack is my son." Turning to Jack, he said, "We are just questioning people as part of our investigation. We don't have any suspects yet." He then went through the same litany of questions that he had done with the others. Finally he asked, "Who unpacked that presentation cornet?"

"Mr. Ritberger did. I was there when he took it out of its crate. He went from the crate to Mr. Stein's bench."

"You saw this?"

"I did. They opened the case together and went over everything."

"Did Stein clean anything?"

"He wiped down the slides and put lubricant on them. Sometimes there is an oily residue on them from being machined at the factory. He took good care of that cornet and then he wiped it clean before putting it back in the case. That's part of the routine for every instrument that goes through the store. The customer is to get a shiny instrument with no smudges or fingerprints when they pick up their new horn. Conn stipulates this to their dealers. It's supposed to have the same excitement as a kid opening a present on Christmas morning."

"Did Stein wipe off the mouthpiece?"

"He would normally do this as the last step, but Mr. Ritberger actually did it this time. The Betsy Ross All-Lady Silver Cornet Band committee requested a Benjamin Bent mouthpiece and he checked to see that the right mouthpiece came in the case. Mr. Ritberger used a soft towel with a little alcohol on it to wipe the mouthpiece down."

"What happened then?"

"Mr. Ritberger carried the case in here. I don't know what happened after it was in this office."

"Have you heard anyone in the store speak ill of Miss Blackthorne?"

"There's a few who grumble about her being uppity. They think that the woman's place is in the home."

"Any names, Jack?"

"One of the fellas plays in the Pick-Penn Company Band. I don't know his name, but his son shoots billiards with Vash . . . er, Miss Smith's brother, Danforth." He was trying to use the polite form of Vashti's name for the record and for his mother who would surely lecture him on good manners, if she heard this from his father.

"Thank you, Jack. You can continue to be of help to us by keeping your ears open and your mouth shut. No one here is a suspect. You may share that, but keep the questions that I have asked and their answers a secret. Back to work, son."

Jack popped up, took one last look around the office, whistled through his teeth and strode back out to the sales floor.

“Well, Brinkman, do you see anything in these interviews that makes you suspicious?”

“All seems to be in order, sir. They would not have known we were coming this morning, so they could not have compared notes. They all answered easily and none of them looks guilty.”

“I think we need to get the name of that bandsman at Pick-Penn. Our next interview should be Mr. Smith, but I don’t want to bring a parade of reporters along with us.

They walked out of the office and into the store. Mr. Ritberger accompanied them to the revolving door and assured O’Brien that they would cooperate in any way that they could.

# Chapter 9

Revolving out the brass doors, the two lawmen found a gaggle of reporters loitering around just as O'Brien has suspected.

"Caught the murderer yet, O'Brien?"

"That's Sgt. O'Brien to you and we have just begun our investigation. We don't have any suspects, boys. We are just gathering information."

"How was she murdered?"

"Now, boys, you know I can't reveal any information like that. As soon as we have information to share you'll get the lowdown from the Roundhouse."

O'Brien and Brinkman climbed into the police wagon and were driven back to the station. For a short while they listened to the clop of the horses hooves on the cobblestone streets.

"I'm not surprised that the reporters followed us. It's a big news story. Miss Blackthorne was such a wonderful lady in our community that I want people to remember her for all the good she did."

Brinkman just listened.

"We'll plan our next interviews when we get back to my office."

Adam nodded and they rode in silence, watching the people on the sidewalks until they got back to the station.

"Whoa, Sam. Whoa, Penny." The wagon came to a halt and the two police men descended from their seats. Walking up the front steps, they were besieged by more reporters. Inside the station there were even more. O'Brien waved off questions, walked through the swinging gate and turned back to the crowd. "Boys, we have just begun our investigation. When there is more information, you will get a statement from our Chief of Police. Now, how about letting us do our work? Go back to your press rooms."

The men grumbled and scuffled out of the station. O'Brien motioned Brinkman into his office, shut the door and hung his cap on the coat tree. "What do you bet they will want to follow us from here on?"

"I would guess that to be their game, sir."

"Well, Patrolman Brinkman, how do we trick them into not following us since it has now become a game?" O'Brien was testing his protégé as he already had a plan in mind.

"I think we split up, Sergeant. They will follow you as the lead investigator. You take them on a wild goose chase and I'll go for the interview at the Smith residence. In the muster room where we meet before going out to walk our beats I will to try to find another patrolman who looks a lot like me. With any luck they won't notice and he can go with you. Then I can walk out the back and go for the interview. That is, if you think this is a good idea, sir."

O'Brien smiled. "Do you know what questions to ask at the Smith residence?" They went over the questions to be asked and Brinkman wrote them all down in a second notebook, leaving the first one in O'Brien's care. Then he went to the muster room to see if there was anyone there who resembled him. With a little luck, the press boys would have paid little attention to him and they'd follow O'Brien when he left through the front door. Who would expect a patrolman to be continuing the investigation? He could go out the back door as if he were walking a beat.

Tom Ralfus was of a similar stature to Brinkman. He had brought in a thug for breaking a window and trying to rob a cigar store overnight. It took a little while to book him and get the paperwork done. Ralfus's night had seemed like the story depicted in D.W. Reeves descriptive entitled *Episodes in a Policeman's Life*. In his head, Brinkman was whistling the musical theme. He made sure this was one of the melodies that he whistled as he walked a beat. It was a good way to pass the time, and it let the children know that he was coming. Any little pranks they might have been scheming were often abandoned before he had to step in to stop them. Brinkman came up and informed him that O'Brien wanted to talk with him. Both patrolmen returned to the Sergeant's office and shut the door. O'Brien detailed the ruse they would use. As they went out the front door, O'Brien would create some bluster for the press while Brinkman walked out the back door and assumed the role of a beat cop. This wasn't hard, as it was his normal role at the precinct. He felt especially valuable to be working on a murder case.

Today, he could actually walk Ralfus's beat and watch to see that no one followed. It would be perfectly natural to him. If he had to, he could walk that beat until they got bored with him. He knew how to cover the city.

So O'Brien took his cap off the coat tree and headed out the front door with Ralfus in tow. "Gather 'round, boys. I'm just headed over to headquarters to consult with the crime laboratory. You all know that Miss Blackthorne was an outstanding citizen of this city. I have been authorized to tell you that we are using all of our resources to solve this murder." At this announcement there was an audible gasp. "I don't have much more for you boys, but you can assure your readers that the Philadelphia Police Force is on the case and that we are putting all of our efforts into this investigation and that we will work tirelessly to apprehend the suspect and to keep our city safe. No questions, boys. I've got to get over to the crime laboratory."

He and Ralfus climbed into the police wagon and he told the driver to take them to headquarters. Sean looked over his shoulder to see if anyone was following them.

"Driver, loop around and go over to the Blackthorne Bunting Works."

Tom Ralfus looked at him. "We'll do some questioning over there. It will be good use of our time.

♫

When the wagon arrived at Blackthorne Bunting Works, they drove through the beautifully crafted wrought iron gates. BBW in stylized letters was at the top of the arch and the letters stood out in gold plate.

This woman had certainly done well for herself, thought Sean. He could imagine that someone would be jealous of her wealth and want to have it.

"Come, Tom. Let's earn our pay."

The two men climbed out of the police wagon and entered the stately building that housed the Blackthorne Bunting Works. Inside it was bright, with many windows allowing natural light onto the production floor. There were rows and rows of women sewing red, white and blue bunting. A few glanced up and a woman of middle age approached them.

"I am Mrs. Sawyer. May I help you gentlemen?"

"Yes, Mrs. Sawyer. I'm Sergeant O'Brien and this is Patrolman Rolfus. Is the manager here today?"

"That would be Mr. Hintz. Here he comes now." She was gesturing toward the back corner of the production floor. A gentleman in a very nice three piece brown suit with a light blue tie was headed their way. He extended his hand to O'Brien,

"Welcome to Blackthorne Bunting Works. I'm Robert Hintz. How may I assist you gentlemen?"

Sean shook his hand first, and while Hintz was shaking hands with Rolfus, said, "We are here about Miss Blackthorne. Is there a place we could speak privately?"

"Certainly. Please follow me." Turning to his floor manager, "Thank you, Mrs. Sawyer." She nodded and went back to her work.

Sean observed the sewers. Their entrance had caused the women all to glance at them, but not one was watching suspiciously. They entered Hintz's office. It was nicely furnished with an oak desk and a matching chair with a red velvet cushion. The walls held patriotic portraits including those of Presidents Washington and Lincoln. Dark blue wallpaper with tiny clusters of white flowers could be seen behind the artwork. O'Brien and Rolfus found chairs in front of the desk and Rolfus drew out his notebook. Hintz sat down and Sean noticed that his chair did not squeak.

"You have, no doubt, surmised that we are investigating Margaret Blackthorne's death."

Hintz put his face in his hands and shook his head. "It is inconceivable to me that anyone would do such a thing to Margaret. She was such a kind soul." He looked up and Sean could see tears welling up in Hintz's eyes.

"How well did you know her?"

"I knew her very well. We grew up next door to one another. She stayed with us when her parents drowned. I have known her my entire life. She was like a sister to me."

"Do you know anyone who would want to hurt her?"

"Let me be very forward about this. Her Last Will and Testament stipulates that a number of her possessions are to pass to me. If I were a greedy man, that would give me motive." He paused to calm himself. "Margaret was always generous to her employees. As her company grew, she hired women from our old neighborhood. They were all immigrant women who were looking for ways to help their families. Margaret's parents had been immigrants. She knew what it was like. She allowed those women to take sewing home so they could watch their children. My own mother was one of those women."

“Now, here I am, the manager of her company. I never dreamed of going this far in life, but Margaret had dreams. My wife and children have a fine life because Margaret believed in me.”

“I was at the concert. I was here at work that day. There are dozens of women out on that floor who can attest to that.”

Sean studied him for a moment. “Did you know that the band had purchased that cornet for her?”

“I did not, but nothing would have pleased her more, except that the band would be a guiding force in the lives of young women. I intend to see to that! I have three girls of my own and I intend to have them all participate in the band as they are old enough.”

O’Brien and Rolfus listened as Hintz poured out his story and, no doubt, his grief. He had risen and was leaning across the desk with his hands laid flat on its surface. He paused and looked around. “Well, will you look at me? I’m unrecognizable! I have always been the soft-spoken type. Here I am pledging to continue her work.”

“It’s alright, Mr. Hintz. This has been a shock to the whole community. We are just looking for leads. I was outside of Founder’s Hall the night of the concert to help with the crowd. Those were very happy people who entered for the cakewalk, but this doesn’t look like an accident. We do suspect murder.”

Hintz put his face back in his hands. “This can’t be happening,” he sighed.

“I’m sorry to put you through this Mr. Hintz, but you would know certain facts that would help us. Do you know who else may have been named in her Last Will and Testament?”

“Her attorney is Mr. Thomas Ryan. He was in New York City on some business for Margaret. I think he will return today. I can give you his address.”

Having obtained the address, O'Brien and Rolfus left the building and climbed into the police wagon. After giving instructions to the driver, Sean turned to Tom. "Well, what do you make of that interview?"

"He's not our man. I've seen lots of families that weren't as close as he and Miss Blackthorne appear to have been. She did right by him. There's no motive."

"That's what I think too. Maybe the attorney will have some information that will help us."

The city was bustling with people getting their errands and shopping done before the heat of mid-day. Goggins was a skilled driver and he knew the city well, so their journey was easily accomplished. He stopped the rig in front of a red brick building with gold-stenciled windows declaring: Thomas Ryan, Attorney at Law.

Alighting from the wagon, the two crossed the sidewalk in a few steps and entered the office. A twenty-something clerk rose from his desk and came their way.

"Good morning, gentlemen."

"Good morning. Is Mr. Ryan in this morning?"

"He is. May I say who's calling?"

"Sergeant O'Brien of the Philadelphia Police Department."

"Very good. Please have a seat," he said, gesturing to a bank of chairs in the office.

The clerk walked to the back of the building. Other clerks in the office were poring over official documents at their desks. There were stacks and stacks of papers and files on every desk. In mere moments Mr. Ryan appeared followed by his clerk.

“Good morning, sirs. Please come to my office.” He turned and retraced his steps with O’Brien and Rolfus following him. “Please have a seat,” he said, gesturing to chairs with beautifully tanned leather.

Sinking into the soft leather, Sean watched Ryan close the door after them. “I can guess why you are here. It’s about Margaret Blackthorne.”

“Yes, sir. It is.”

“I am not allowed to show you her Last Will & Testament until said document is read. However, I will probably be able to answer some questions.” Ryan’s green eyes focused on Sean.
“It would assist us a great deal. Thank you.”

“Miss Blackthorne leaves quite a large estate. The bulk of that estate is left in a trust. There isn’t one particular person who would benefit from her death. In death, as in life, she took care of everyone around her.”

“That gets right to the point, Mr. Ryan. It clarifies any questions I would have for the moment. Should you think of anyone or anything else that could help in our investigation, please contact the District One station.”

Their brief conversation concluded, O’Brien and Rolfus took their leave. Goggins was taking care of his team when the two men came out of the office. “Back to the station, Goggins.” Looking at Rolfus, O’Brien said, “Maybe Brinkman will be back and we can compare our notes.”

# Chapter 10

Vashti sat sniffling and dabbing her nose daintily with her hankie. She'd had a good cry and was at the window in her bedroom tracing the lace curtains with her eyes. Beyond the white lace, trees were in bloom. She could see the children across the street rolling a large hoop with a stick, but inside her room there was a debate running in her brain. Should she concoct a story about needing something at the Conn store? How would she get to the store without a chaperone? A real lady didn't travel about all alone. If she did get to the store, how would she talk to Jack in private? There seemed to be no easy answer. Maybe she should just come right out and ask her parents to help her. She felt useless just sitting at home waiting for the next newsprint edition to come out with the latest information on Miss Blackthorne's murder.

From the downstairs hallway she could hear a knock at the front door and Hettie's shuffling walk on the way to answer. She heard people talking and her father's voice calling upstairs. "Danforth, please come downstairs." That seemed strange. Who would be calling on Danforth? She walked out of her room and to the landing at the top of the stairs gazing down at the front entryway. There was a police patrolman, her father and Danforth, whose feet were just parting the stairs. Danforth reached out to shake hands with the patrolman who gave him a big smile, shifted his hat to his left hand and grasped the extended greeting warmly.

Why was there a policeman in their house? Why did he want to speak to Danforth? Why? Why? Why? She caught her father's eye. He motioned with his head for her to go back to her room. This she did right away. Although the suspense was killing her, she knew that her father would share what he could later.

Mr. Smith led Danforth and Patrolman Brinkman into his study and closed the door. He motioned for the two friends to sit and went behind his desk, as well.

"I'm guessing that you are here about Miss Blackthorne. Is that right, Adam?"

"Yes, sir, it is. I'm helping with the investigation. There's a mob of reporters at the station. Sgt. O'Brien is keeping them busy so they wouldn't follow me here. We wouldn't want a crowd on your doorstep."

"That's very thoughtful of the department. Thank you. What do you need of us?"

"I have some questions for you and Danforth. You aren't a suspect, Danforth. We are just trying to piece together as much information as possible and I must ask you both to keep this conversation confidential."

Danforth and Mr. Smith nodded that they both understood.

"Mr. Smith, I'll start with you. You had the cornet here in your home. Is that right?"

"Yes, it is. My wife and daughter picked it up from the Conn store on Wednesday morning. The previous night Jack O'Brien came by to let us know that it had arrived."

"Did they bring it directly back here?"

"Yes, they did."

"Where was it kept?" he asked while writing notes in his logbook.

"Right here on my desk," he said tapping the top of the desk with his index finger.

"Could anyone have tampered with it?"

"It was wrapped in heavy brown paper when my wife and Vashti brought it to the house. We were trying to keep it a secret and the shiny new case would have given it away, so it was wrapped at the store and kept that way until a few minutes before we left for the concert. I took the paper off myself and Danforth carried the cornet."

He then related how he and his son had worked out a scheme so that Miss Blackthorne would not be backstage to see the cornet and spoil the surprise.

Brinkman turned to Danforth and asked, "What did you do with the case while you were at the billiard hall?"

Danforth stared at his shoes. He was feeling sheepish, but he looked at Brinkman and gave him a straight-forward answer. "I set it down in the back room when I went to play a quick game with Casswell." He paused a moment and then asked Brinkman, "Do you think someone at the billiard parlor tampered with the cornet?"

"We don't know, Danforth. We are just gathering information. Who else was in that back room?"

"The back room has the best billiard table and is reserved for the best players. Casswell and Starkie were there when I walked in. I was just going to watch, but, . . . well, you know how these things go. I know that Bob Matthis was there and Howard Ritchie, Sven Torgalson and Randy Brewer. I wasn't paying much attention to the rest of the crowd with my mind on the game."

"Was the cornet ever out of your sight?"

"It was for a period of ten to fifteen minutes. I had set it against the back wall and the crowd was packed in there mighty tight. They try to give us plenty of room for the cue stick. When I discovered the time, I had to push my way through to get to my coat and the cornet."

"Was it in the same place or did it appear to have been moved?"

"I think it was in the same place, but I don't know for certain."

"Danforth, are those fellas usually at the billiard parlor on Friday evenings?"

“Most of them are. Carson’s is the place for the sharpest players and that’s usually Fridays. Matthis, Ritchie, Torgalson and Brewer are in there most weekday evenings too, if you are looking for them.”

“Can either of you think of anyone who had it in for Miss Blackthorne?”

“Casswell gripes about her once in a while. His father works for Pick-Penn and plays in the company band. He’s always trying to talk smart about things his pop says about Miss Blackthorne and the girl’s band.”

“Anyone else?”

Neither father or son could come up with any other names. They both shook their heads no.

“Mr. Smith, would your daughter know anything that might help us in our investigation?”

“I doubt it, but you may question her. I will, of course, be present.”

“Certainly. I would like to talk to her.”

“Danforth, please go and tell your sister to come to my study.” He dismissed his son who left the room, closing the door behind him. While he ran up the stairs to Vashti’s room, Brinkman and Mr. Smith talked about the weather, Brinkman’s family and how he liked his work on the police force.

Upstairs Danforth tapped on his sister’s door. “Vashti, Adam Brinkman wants to talk to you,” he said quietly and a little out of breath. She opened the door and said, “Is this about Miss Blackthorne?”

“Yes. Brinkman’s working the case and he’s just gathering information right now.”

"So that's Adam Brinkman. I thought he looked familiar." She was looking in her mirror to see if her hair was presentable. A quick rub of her splotchy face and she was ready. She closed her door behind her and headed down the staircase behind Danforth. He knocked on the door of their father's study and waited. "Come in."

He opened the door for his sister and then looked at Brinkman with raised eyebrows in his mother's questioning gesture. Brinkman waved him off. Danforth closed the door, wishing he could hear what was being said.

Both men rose from their seats as Vashti entered the room and waited for her to be seated before sitting down again.

Brinkman smiled kindly at her. "We are gathering information about last night. I know that you were close to Miss Blackthorne and that this is all very difficult. Anything you can tell us might help to solve this case."

Vashti's eyes welled up with tears, but she blinked them back and gathered herself again.

"Miss Smith, do you know anyone who might have had a grudge against Miss Blackthorne?"

Vashti sighed. This was so difficult. She was glad that she knew Adam Brinkman. He and Danforth had played together when they were younger. He had nice eyes. Smiling at him, she said, "I know that there are people who don't like the band. They might not have liked Miss Blackthorne either, but I don't know any names."

"How do you know they don't like the band?"

"Some of the ladies in the band have told stories of things that they have overheard from their neighbors or at various social affairs. We always tried not to talk about these things too much. Idle gossip is not very becoming to ladies." She flashed him a wonderful smile.

Focusing his attention on his notebook, he asked, "Do you know any names?"

“I don’t, but Jack O’Brien works at the Conn store and he might. He hears quite a lot of band news at the store.”

“Do you know if anyone other than Miss Blackthorne touched the cornet?”

“I don’t, but you can tell from looking at it. I am forever wiping down my French horn. Everywhere you touch a brass instrument there’s a smudge. A silver cornet like that one would have lots of smudges.”

This was news to Brinkman. He had played alto horn in the Kendelton Boy’s Band, but he never worried about finger marks on his old horn. He’d have to get back to the station and let O’Brien know.

“Anything else you can think of?”

She shook her head no and he liked the way that the curls danced around her face.

He tried to give her a sympathetic, reassuring smile. “Thank you both. Please, do not talk to anyone about my being here and asking questions. We don’t want to jeopardize the investigation.” Picking up his hat from its resting place at his feet, he rose to leave. Mr. Smith and Vashti did likewise and followed him out of the study and to the front foyer. Brinkman peeked out to see if any reporters had tailed him. Not a one was in sight.

“Thank you again.” He opened the front door, stepped on to the front stoop, placed his patrolman’s hat on his head and hit the pavement for another half an hour as a beat cop. Then he walked back to the station and entered through the back door.

# Chapter 11

"Father, I know he said we shouldn't talk to anyone about this, but I can talk to you, can't I?"

"Well, Vashti, I think you and I can talk, and Danforth, too. I will tell your mother. Husbands and wives often have confidences among themselves. She'll be careful not to spread any rumors. Your mother is a very smart person. It's one of the things that I love about her. I will sit Reggie down and explain what has happened and why we won't speak about this at dinner. Hettie knows the police were here and I'll ask her not to say anything to anyone as well. She'll be good about it. She's practically part of the family. This is a kind way of not involving them unnecessarily. This is very serious business." They both sat in silence thinking through the developments of the last hour or so. Mr. Smith put his hand on his daughter's shoulder. "I would suggest that you go to your room and wait there until I call you."

Vashti left her father's study and slowly ascended the stairs. Her thoughts were as jumbled as a band mixing up their jump over endings in a march. She had to talk to Jack!

Brinkman walked casually to O'Brien's office just in case there were any reporters lurking around in the public space. The coast was clear.

"May I speak with you, Sgt. O'Brien?" he intoned in his most cheery voice. O'Brien was waiting for him and the air was electric with anticipation. "Certainly, Brinkman. Come in."

♫

The front doorbell went *zshing*! Vashti knew it must be her friends, but she allowed Hettie to answer the door. Christina and Sadie entered the vestibule talking all at once with Hettie. It sounded like a grand fugue. Emotions *crescendoed* and *decrescendoed* through the air, their voices tense and strained with talk of the shocking news about Miss Blackthorne. Earlier that morning Vashti had received a notecard by the morning post informing her that Christina and her mother would be visiting later that morning.

"Isn't it awful? No one in my family can comprehend why such a horrible thing could happen to such a nice lady," staccatoed Christina. Sadie was all dewy-eyed, but bobbled her head in agreement and sniffed.

Vashti had her pocketbook and was at the door talking with Christina and offering a gentle hug to Sadie. Christina's mother was waiting in their carriage. The three band women marched out of the house, Vashti kissing her mother's cheek with a promise to behave well.

Mrs. Smith gave a wave to Mrs. Swenson. On a grave day such as this one, one would be forgiven the breach of etiquette of not stopping to visit with the lady of the house for a polite half an hour of conversation and tea. Scrambling down the steps to the carriage, the three friends were filled with emotion over the passing of Miss Blackthorne. "Who would want to murder Miss Blackthorne?" said Christina. "She did so much for the community and for women."

"There are men in this city who will be happy she isn't organizing women anymore," shared Vashti. "We loved her, but there are men and women who don't think young ladies should play band instruments."

"Why would anyone think that?" bobbled Sadie. "Playing music is an art!"

"Oh, Sadie, hasn't anyone ever made fun of you for playing the tuba?" intoned Christina. "It took a while for my parents to warm up to the fact that I wanted to be in a band. Piccolo was an okay choice of instrument, but I can't imagine what they would have said if I had asked to play the trombone." Mrs. Swenson was right there for this conversation, but her English wasn't very good. She was sad about Miss Blackthorne, but not as emotionally tied to the situation.

"I want to talk to Jack about the investigation," Vashti stated with intent and purpose. "Maybe he knows more details. I also think that all of the band members need to be vigilant. We don't know if any of us could be next."

Christina sat bolt upright. "I hadn't thought of that."

Sadie was still dewy-eyed, but she was intent on finding the culprit as well. Miss Blackthorne had been so wonderful about teaching her to play the tuba. She never felt like a misfit with gangly limbs around Miss Blackthorne. Instead she learned to love that big piece of brass and revel in the noble bass lines written by the world's greatest composers for it.

# Chapter 12

Brinkman walked in, closed the door and waited for the reassuring sound of the latch. He sat down and looked at O'Brien, who quizzed him, "Anyone follow you, or did we fool them?"

"We fooled them, sir. I don't think anyone is wise to us."

O'Brien gave a tummy laugh and smiled to himself. He knew that the reporters were just trying to do their jobs, but sometimes it was a game and he enjoyed when he could win a round or two.

"What did you learn at the Smith home?"

"Two important things, sir. I have the name of the billiard player whose father has been bad-mouthing Miss Blackthorne. It's William Casswell. He can be found at Carson's Billiard Parlor most nights of the week."

"Good work, Brinkman! What's the second thing?"

"Miss Smith said something interesting. She said that there might be smudges on the silver cornet if someone other than Miss Blackthorne touched it. I think she means fingerprints. I played alto horn myself, but my instrument was just brass. I never thought about fingerprints. Do you think Dr. Harrison might be able to get some fingerprints off the cornet?"

O'Brien nodded. Brinkman had done some very good police work this morning. Back in his cornet playing days, Sean's cornet had a finish called silver satin. It didn't show wear and was especially liked by the repairmen because they could take out dents without the hammer marks showing in the metal. He'd learned that at the supper table when Jack was talking about fixing band instruments.

"That could shed some light on this case if he could. We haven't used that kind of scientific evidence very much, but I think the Doc has the knowledge to do it. I'll call over to the morgue."

O'Brien stood up and left the office. In the outer room he asked the dispatcher to call over to Doc Harrison's. Spinning on his heel, he returned to the office.

"After we hear from the Doc we should find Casswell and talk to his father. Doc said the poison was arsenic. We should check with drug stores in the area to see if they have any record of someone purchasing arsenic. They are required by law to keep a register of poisons purchased."

"I think that arsenic is usually used by farmers to get rid of pests, but we will, in all probability, need to know more about its usage. I've never had a murder case like this before, but I recall listening to stories from the older men on the force."

The telephone rang and O'Brien picked it up. "Glad that I got to you, Doc. Would you look at the cornet to see if there are any fingerprints? I'll wait." O'Brien rested the earpiece on his shoulder waiting for the Doc. "There are. Great. Do you think you can get fingerprints from Miss Blackthorne's body? Right. Call me when you have something." He put the earpiece back in the cradle and placed the telephone on his desk. "Brinkman, use the city directory to find the closest drug stores. Go out the back again and check on the poison registers. You're doing a great job on this case. Keep it up."

"Yes, sir. Thank you, sir."

Brinkman stood up and ambled out to the front desk where the dispatchers were and where the directories were kept. He found the three closest drug stores and wrote their addresses down in his patrolman's notebook. A little quick calculation told him that he could walk to all three in the next couple of hours. Before leaving, he returned to O'Brien's office. "Sergeant, is it alright if I stop for lunch? Might look a little more normal if someone is watching me."

“Good idea. Go right ahead.”

“Thank you, sir.”

O’Brien was pleased to have Brinkman working the case. He hadn’t counted on this, but the young man was sharp. He heard a little commotion in the front of the station and looked out to see his son George bringing his lunch. George peeked in to the office. “Well, son, what kind of tasty lunch did you bring me today?”

♫

Brinkman made a concerted effort not to walk fast, whistling another section from “Episodes in a Policeman’s Life.” He left the station and walked a parallel route to his first destination. That way he could check to see if there was a reporter following him. Those newspapermen would be getting restless. This was a big story with Miss Blackthorne having been such a pillar of the community. He figured that the honeymoon would soon be over with the press.

Turning a corner, he stopped to talk to a storekeeper who was setting out more produce. With a little polite banter he could watch to see if anyone was on his tail. Tapping his hat with his billy-club, he walked a few more blocks talking to people along the way. With a left turn he walked up to his first destination. The screen door had a bell that tinkled when he entered. Rassmusen’s was a combination soda fountain, small hardware and drug store. There were a few people sitting at the counter. Talking his hat off he greeted those who looked up with a smile and a nod. A man in a dark suit was at the back of the store. He stood and approached Brinkman. “Good afternoon, officer. May I help you?”

“Good afternoon. Are you Mr. Rassmusen?”

“I am.”

“Is there a place we could talk privately?”

“Yes. Please, follow me.”

Rassmusen turned and led the way to his office. Brinkman noted that the office was as tidy as the store. He was sure he would get accurate information here. Rassmusen closed the door. "How may I help you?"

"I would like to see your poison register."

"Right away. I'll be back in a moment."

He left the office and Brinkman took a look around. It was a small but efficient space that was well organized. Shelves were built from floor to ceiling and lined with catalogs for various kinds of merchandise. A coat tree held a black bowler hat. Rassmusen returned with the register under his arm. Closing the door, he took a seat at his desk, pulled out the shelf that served as an extra workspace and laid the register on the shelf, turning it so Brinkman could read it. "Have you seen one of these before, officer?"

Brinkman had enough sense to admit he had not. Using his powers of detection, he could see that Rassmusen was about to educate him. "I have not."

"We are required to keep a record of any chemicals that we sell. You'll see here a list of inventory when we purchase a drug. If we sell that drug, it goes into the register. In this way the drugs are always accounted for. Do you know what drug you are looking for?"

"I am looking for anyone who purchased arsenic."

"We have not had an arsenic purchase in three years. If you turn the page back you'll see a gentleman listed who purchased arsenic. He is a farmer and was trying to get rid of rodents. Arsenic was not detectable for many years and it became known as 'inheritance powder'. Hundreds of years ago it was easy to kill someone using arsenic and it couldn't be detected. That's one of the reasons why we now have to keep this register. Has someone been poisoned?"

Brinkman looked at him, but did not reply.

"You don't have to answer and I will be quite discreet. You should know that one of the byproducts of smelting is arsenic. In addition to checking out the local druggists, you should visit the smelters in the area."

"Smelting? Really? Thank you, Mr. Rassmusen. You have been very helpful." He stood up, shook this druggist's hand and headed for the front door. The little bell tinkled as he hit the sidewalk. Thoughts raced through his head. Smelting. Another arrow was pointing to Pick-Penn.

There was now a persistent rumble in his belly. The Horn & Hardart was just a couple of blocks away at 818 Chestnut Street. He could stop at the police callbox on the next corner to let the dispatcher know he was going to stop for his noon meal. Evans would let O'Brien know where he was and would update him on any further developments if necessary.

After calling the station he walked the next block, entered the restaurant and took his cap off. The men who owned their own businesses usually went home for their midday meal. This place was always buzzing with shoppers and workers. The counter had only fifteen stools, but people ate quickly and one could usually get a seat. He would have a cup of coffee and a roast beef sandwich that came with a dill pickle.

Horn & Hardart was known for their New Orleans-style coffee. It was blended with chicory. The signs in the store hailed it as their "gilt-edge" brew. It was strong, but smooth.

To his surprise he noted Daniel O'Toole and Jack O'Brien having their meal together. Their eyes met and he nodded hello, but did not go over to talk. He found a stool at the other end of the counter, ate quickly and resumed his task.

The next two drug stores came up empty. Their poison logs were well-kept, but there were no recent records of anyone purchasing arsenic. When he was within a couple blocks of the police station, he could see reporters milling around. Brinkman set his feet to the back entrance, but there were a couple of reporters back there, too.

“Sad thing this business with Miss Blackthorne, ain’t it,” one of them offered trying to work up a conversation.

“Yes, it is, but I don’t know anything to help you out, boys. Sgt. O’Brien will be the one to let you know when he has more news.

“We was hoping for a scoop, officer.”

“Sorry, boys, I can’t help you.” With that he was through the back door of the station. It would be harder from here on in to keep the reporters at bay. Brinkman thought to himself that it was good they had gotten to the Smith household before the reporters had caught on. Walking to the front of the station, he could see more reporters loitering around the front lobby. At O’Brien’s office he stopped and rapped on the doorframe. O’Brien motioned for him to enter and close the door.

“What’s the state of reporters in the back?”

“There’s a couple of them by the rear entrance, trying to wheedle out information.”

“They are getting restless. Nothing we can do about it, just get this crime solved. What did you find out?”

“I have a little more information. None of the drug stores has sold any arsenic recently. One sold some three years ago to a farmer who was using it to rid himself of pests. I did get a good piece of information from one of the druggists. He told me that arsenic is a side product of smelting. Wasn’t one of the band grumblers an employee at Pick-Penn Smelting and Iron Works?”

Leaning back in his squeaky chair O’Brien stroked his chin. “Hmm. I believe you are right.” Picking up Brinkman’s first notebook, he flipped through the pages. “Here it is. Danforth Smith shoots billiards with the son of a Pick-Penn employee who has groused about Miss Blackthorne and the ladies' band. We don't have a first name for the man, just Casswell. Well, let's go visit the factory and see if we can interview this man. We'll go together and use a driver and wagon this time. The press will try to follow, but maybe we can surprise them and throw them off a bit."

He grabbed his hat, swung the door open and was out the front door with Brinkman on his heels. "Evans, I'll check in. Likely gone for a while."

"Yes, sir."

"Got a break in the case, Sergeant?" The reporters were suddenly on their feet scrambling to ask questions.

"We're just following a lead, boys. Nothing concrete yet."

He was down the front steps and the reporters outside were jumping up, too. "Nothing yet, boys." He strode to the first police wagon, climbed up and told the driver to head south. Pick-Penn was actually north, but they might lose a few would-be followers this way. Even if the reporters had a wagon available, they'd have to get into it to follow.

"Take a few random turns, driver. Try to lose 'em if they follow." Sean took a quick glance over his shoulder and, seeing no one following, said, "Take us to Pick-Penn Smelting & Iron Works. You know where it is?"

"Yes, sir."

They drove for about fifteen minutes and then pulled up at the front gate of the factory. The horses were breathing a little heavily. A guard came out of the gatehouse. "Good afternoon, sirs. How can I help you?"

"We would like to speak with the owner."

"He's not here, sir. The supervisor, Mr. Kitridge, is in. May I tell him who is calling?" He was picking up the telephone inside the gatehouse.

"Sgt. O'Brien from the Philadelphia Police Department."

They waited while the guard called the office. He walked back to the wagon. "They will be expecting you at the main office. Drive through the gate and then turn right. You'll see the office entrance."

The wagon pulled ahead, turned, and they were at the door. O'Brien and Brinkman leapt out of the wagon and walked up the steps to the main office. As they entered they took off their hats and directed their attention to the young man at the desk.

"I'm Sgt. O'Brien and this is Patrolman Brinkman. We're here to see Mr. Kitridge."

The young man stood and started toward a large oak door. "Right this way gentlemen. Mr. Kitridge is waiting for you." With that he opened the door and showed them in. The oriental carpet was a jumble of colors, mostly greens and reds. Over the fireplace mantle was a model of a three masted schooner. Its name, Hermoine, was painted on the stern. The artwork around the room ran towards sailing and hunting. Kitridge was emerging from behind his desk.

"Good afternoon, officers. How may I be of service to you?" His arm was outstretched and his handshake was strong, but not like a vise. He was a man in his 50s or early 60s. His hair was brown and slightly graying at the temples. His suit was charcoal gray and his tie stud was a lustrous pearl.

"Mr. Kitridge, I am Sgt. O'Brien and this is Patrolman Brinkman. I appreciate you seeing us on short notice. We are in the midst of a murder investigation and hope you can help us."

"My goodness!" His hands were suddenly grasping the lapels of his charcoal gray suit and tugging mindlessly. His bushy eyebrows showed great concern as they rose and fell with his distressed eyes, first one eyebrow and then the other. "Of course. Please, sit down."

He motioned to sturdy chairs with maroon leather cushions, his fingers flapping a bit. They all sat and Brinkman brought out his notebook.

“Do you have an employee named Casswell? We think he plays in the company band.”

“My, heavens! Did he kill someone? Oh, this isn’t good.” He was alternately wringing his hands and tugging on the lapels of his suit. “I don’t like this. Bad publicity for the company, my heavens! A murderer on the loose!” More hand wringing and lapel pulling ensued before he refocused on the two policemen. “I do not know of this person, but I’ll find out for you.” He stood, walked to his desk, picked up the telephone and grabbed the earpiece from the cradle. He clicked the cradle a couple of times. “Mr. Young, please bring me a list of all of the band members.” He returned the earpiece to the cradle, sat the telephone back on his desk and returned to his seat. “You’ll have it shortly.”

“I understand that one of the side products of smelting is arsenic. Is that correct?”

“Yes, it is.”

“Can you tell me what you do with that product?”

“Certainly. Arsenic is most often a side product from the purification of copper and lead. It will also be found in the process of purifying gold, but we don’t do any of that work at this facility. The coke ovens produce something called metallic arsenic. This is often used to increase the strength of items made of either copper or lead. It’s actually a different kind of arsenic than what the druggists use. It would not have the same effect.”

Mr. Young entered the office and handed a list of musicians to Mr. Kitridge. He handed the list back to Mr. Young. “Can you look? I’m too upset to look myself. My heavens, I could not bear it. Not here at Pick-Penn! Sergeant, what name was it?”

Mr. Young scanned down the first page and flipped the top sheet to the back. “I see here that we do have a Henry Casswell playing clarinet in the band. Would you like for him to be brought here?”

“We’re so sorry to disturb you and the factory, but, yes, we would like to question him. But discreetly. No one must know, Mr. Kitridge. We must keep this very quiet.”

Tugging his lapels, “Mr. Young, please have Mr. Casswell brought to my office.”

“Yes, sir.” Young was quickly gone.

Kitridge continued his talk on the way things were smelted and how they gathered up the metallic arsenic. In a short time there was a knock on the door.

“Come in.”

The door opened and Mr. Young showed a dirty, raggedy man into the office. He had white skin around his eyes where he had been wearing glasses. It was obvious that he was ill at ease. It was extremely rare to be called into the office of the supervisor. He couldn’t imagine what he’d done wrong.

“You are Henry Casswell?” The worker nodded. “These officers have some questions for you. Sgt. O’Brien, I’ll leave you here and will just be outside if you need anything.”

“Thank you, Mr. Kitridge.”

Kitridge left the office and O’Brien took a long look at Casswell, sizing him up. “Mr. Casswell, do you play in the Pick-Penn Company Band?”

“I do.”

“And do you enjoy this endeavor?”

“I do.”

"Where do you work in the factory?"

"I work in the crusher. The iron ore comes in and it has to be crushed before going to the blast furnace."

"Where were you last Friday night?"

"I finished my shift here at the factory about 5 o'clock. Then I went home and had my dinner and was with my family."

"Have you ever heard the Betsy Ross All-Lady Silver Cornet Band?"

"I have not."

"Did you know Margaret Blackthorne?"

"No, sir, not personally."

"Never saw her from a distance or the band from a distance?"

"No sir." He was sweating, but he didn't seem to know anything about the band or Miss Blackthorne. He wasn't showing any signs of being nervous or avoiding eye contact. Brinkman wasn't sure he even knew that Margaret Blackthorne was dead.

"Word on the street is that you were bad mouthing Miss Blackthorne. Any truth to that rumor?"

Casswell squirmed a bit and shifted on his feet. "I might have complained about her once or twice."

"What did you say, Mr. Casswell?"

He was clearly uncomfortable now. O'Brien didn't think he was the killer, but he thought he'd just pursue this line of questioning a little further.

"Well?" he encouraged.

"I think I may have complained about her putting crazy ideas in all those girls' heads. What kind of woman plays in a band? That's for men." He was getting a little agitated.

"So you do know of Miss Blackthorne and her ladies' band." Casswell shifted his feet and stared down at his shoes. "Tell us the truth, Mr. Casswell, it will go much easier for you." Casswell said nothing. "You do know that Miss Blackthorne was murdered last Friday evening."

Casswell stumbled backward like he had been hit in the chest. He shook his head and blurted out, "I, I didn't know that! I didn't have nothing to do with it!" He was clearly scared.

"Can you prove you were here and then at your home?"

"The overseer in the crusher can tell you I was here and my wife can tell you I was at home."

"Anyone besides your wife know you were at home?"

"Sure, lots of folks. In the summer when it's hot like this we all sit on the front steps to stay as cool as we can at night. There must be twenty neighbors who could tell you I was there."

"Alright, Mr. Casswell. Calm down. We're just checking out leads. Don't talk about this to anyone. That will be all for now. You can return to your work."

Casswell turned and headed out the door as fast as he could go.

"I don't think it's him, Brinkman. How about you?"

"I don't think he even knew about Miss Blackthorne. He seemed genuinely surprised to hear about her death."

"I think we are done here. We can always chase down his neighbors if something changes."

The two men walked out of the office to find Mr. Kitridge seated in his own outer office with Mr. Young working at his desk.

"We have completed our interview. Thank you for your help and for the use of your office. We are most likely done here. Would you watch Mr. Casswell's work habits for the next three or four days? If he doesn't show up for work, call the station and ask for me."

Mr. Kitridge had bounced to his feet and was shifting from one foot to another. "I will be happy to do that. Mr. Young, make a note of that, please."

They shook hands and walked out of the building. The wagon took them back to the station where the reporters were milling about again. Taking the lead, O'Brien leapt down from the wagon and headed up the front steps. "No news, boys. We eliminated a potential suspect. We're just following our leads. You could tell your readers that much. Maybe you could also tell them that they should contact the police if they have a lead. Thanks."

At that, he and Brinkman were through the front doors into his office and were about to close the office door when Evans said, "Sir, I have a communication here just in from the coroner." He handed it to O'Brien who entered his office and tossed it on the desk. He hung up his hat and coat, gestured for Brinkman to do the same and settled himself in his squeaky chair to read the note. He looked up at Brinkman. "Doc says there is only one set of prints on the mouthpiece and they belong to Miss Blackthorne."

"Didn't Morty put the cornet in its case? There should be another set of prints."

"Not necessarily" offered Brinkman.

"What do you mean?"

"Sergeant, it says that there is only one set of prints on the *mouthpiece*. That's a Conn Wonder cornet. The Doc could have put the cornet in the case without touching the mouthpiece. In that style of cornet case the mouthpiece can be left in and the cover closed. He wouldn't have had to touch the mouthpiece at all."

"If that doesn't beat all! So what we have here is a murdered woman. We know the cornet is the murder weapon and that there are only the victim's prints on the cornet and the mouthpiece. We don't know where the arsenic came from and we have no motive. How's that for a fine day of police work!" Brinkman could appreciate the frustration.

"Well, sir, we have crossed off some people from the possible list of suspects."

"You are right, Brinkman. At least for now. Miss Blackthorne was such a socially prominent person." He rubbed his forehead and let air out slowing, puffing his cheeks. "The community will want answers and they will want them soon. They will want to know that this monster isn't a threat to anyone else, too."

"What other leads do we have?"

"Unless we check out smelters and druggists farther away, we are back to Conn. I hate to go in there and have the press following, but we may have no choice. I'll have to order Doc to release that body soon. The community will want to mourn. I need some answers! I personally need some answers!" He shouted in frustration. "If someone is going around randomly poisoning brass players, I need to know this." He looked at Brinkman. "Maybe she wasn't the one targeted. Maybe she was the one who accidently got that cornet." He rubbed his forehead again. "Is someone trying to finger Casswell? Is someone going after the Conn store or Mr. Ritberger? What is happening here? I need answers!"

He stroked his chin thinking through what they knew. "Let's go home, Adam. A good rest away from the case may give us a new perspective."

So the two men gathered their hats and coats. Brinkman walked to the ready room. Here he changed his clothes. This was his routine each day. Then he was truly off-duty.

Sean picked up the phone and called Evans's desk requesting that he come into the office. When he entered and closed the door behind him Sean said, "Evans, call over to the morgue and give permission to release the body."

"Yes, sir. I believe that a Mr. Hintz has been asking that very question. He is employed by Blackthorne Bunting Works."

"Please put a note to that effect on my desk with his phone number. That will be a priority for us first thing in the morning."

"Yes, sir."

Sean gathered his hat and coat and walked out through the reporters who were tossing staccato questions at him like timpani strokes in Verdi's *Anvil Chorus*. He just waved them off and started home with questions of his own crossing his brain like an open stroke roll.

# Chapter 13

Richard went out to the mailbox for the afternoon delivery. There was a postcard for Vashti, which he resisted the temptation to read. "Vashti, you have a postcard," he said to his daughter who was in the parlor.

She ran out to the front foyer with a smile on her fresh young face and her brown curls bouncing. "Thank you, father." She took the card into the parlor where her mother was doing embroidery. She read:

**Dear Vashti,**

**I think the Betsy Ross All-Ladies Silver Cornet Band should be involved, at the very least, in a tribute to Miss Blackthorne. I am inviting you to my home tomorrow at 10:00 a.m. to make those plans. Today I have also written to the Blackthorne Bunting Works to ask how we could be a part of the funeral. I do not know if any plans have already been made.**

**Yours,**

**Amanda Fetkenheuer**

Vashti looked up at her parents. "It's from Amanda. She's asked me to be a part of a planning committee for a tribute to Miss Blackthorne. They are meeting at her house tomorrow at 10:00 a.m. I would very much like to do this. May I?"

Elizabeth looked to Richard and nodded. She knew he would say "yes" and the two of them always strove to present a united front.

"You certainly may and I will take you there myself. It will be good for me to get outside and not spend all day studying literature. I remember well the proverb of James Howell, 'All work and no play makes Jack a dull boy'." He smiled at his daughter. She was handling the loss of Miss Blackthorne reasonably well. In fact, it seemed like the ladies of the Betsy Ross All-Ladies Silver Cornet Band were about to make Miss Blackthorne proud one more time.

♫

Sean entered the O'Brien home to the sound of happy children. As was his custom, he plopped his hat on the head of the nearest O'Brien child, pulling it down over the chosen one's eyes, much to their delight. His children were such a joy to him and he played with them while Molly put the finishing touches on their supper. He had smelled boiled cabbage as he walked past all of the open front windows in the neighborhood. It seemed like every family was having boiled cabbage tonight. For as many Irish as there were in this neighborhood, they certainly might be.

Soon enough Molly called the clan to supper with an admonition for all to wash their hands before coming to the table. When they were all seated at the table they said grace and began a happy mealtime together. Sean asked all of the children about their day. Everyone listened, and they had been taught to ask questions. George often had a joke or a riddle to tell. The meal completed, Sean helped Molly with the dishes and Rachel and Jack watched their siblings.

As the evening wore on, the younger children were bathed and put to bed. No mention was made of the Sergeant's visit to the Conn store, but Jack's brain was buzzing with questions. Eventually it was just Molly, Sean and Jack sitting at the table. "Pop, I thought you might like to know that Mr. Ritberger sent a telegram to Mr. Conn informing him of Miss Blackthorne's death. She's been a huge topic of conversation at the store, but it doesn't seem like anyone knows anything."

"Thanks, Jack. I appreciate that information. You may tell Mr. Ritberger that I had the coroner release the body to the funeral home. I would think that the funeral will be scheduled very soon. Does Mr. Ritberger know you are my son?"

"I told him, Pop. I think he actually knew before. Maybe Daniel told him. He certainly would have seen us together at the cakewalk."

"Hmm. That's true. Well, keep your ears open. Hadn't you best be getting to bed, Jack?"

Jack stood up, pushed his chair back under the table, gave his mother a kiss on the cheek and wished his parents a good night. When he was gone, Molly looked at her handsome husband. She already knew the answer, but asked anyway, "Well, Sean?"

"Nothing, Molly. We've eliminated a few things and people, be we have no motive and no suspects. We'll dig deeper tomorrow.

# Chapter 14

Vashti was awake early. Her thoughts were many and jumbled one after another. Why did this have to happen to Miss Blackthorne? Who could have been so cruel? What would happen to the band and all of the friends she had made in the band? She could hardly wait to see her girl friends. They had so much to talk about. Dressing carefully in her favorite shirtwaist and a powder gray skirt, she added a red belt to brighten her outfit. It was Miss Blackthorne's favorite color. Only family members wore black for mourning. With a tap on her door her mother entered and offered to do her hair. Vashti loved to have her mother brush out her hair. Her rebellious curls would behave for her mother. Once she had her hair brushed out, they went downstairs to breakfast.

Richard was at the table reading the morning edition of the newspaper. Danforth was reading the second section and Reggie was looking at a book about larvae. "Not much news in the paper. Tentative plans for the funeral are that it will be held on Saturday at 1:00 p.m. Bishop Thadeus Beecher presiding. They are expecting to have more details for the evening edition of the newspaper."

Breakfast was accomplished efficiently and Richard said he would get his hat. Her mother pinned Vashti's hat on as well. She knew that Vashti hated hats, but she had managed to teach her daughter that a lady wore a hat to keep her skin out of the sun. "Let's go, Vashti. Goodbye, my dear." He kissed his wife and they were out the door, down the steps and walking along the sidewalk to the PRT.

"I'm glad to be doing something constructive, Father. It's maddening not to be able to find the vicious person who murdered Miss Blackthorne! I know it isn't my job to find that person, but I feel so helpless sitting at home doing nothing! It's wonderful that Amanda is taking the lead here. Miss Blackthorne loved all of her band members, but I think that Amanda held a special place in her heart. Amanda is such a gifted musician and with Miss Blackthorne playing the cornet, too, they were great friends."

As they walked on, Vashti chattered on like the accompaniment part to a Wilbur Sweetman rag. Richard was happy to listen to his daughter talk. He knew that this was a tragedy in all of the young ladies' lives and he was especially hopeful that she could manage her grief. She was a little more reserved on the PRT, but prattled once they were walking again.

Amanda lived in a nice brownstone with her Fetkenheuer grandparents, her mother and father and her siblings. Her grandfather had been a concert pianist in Germany and still taught a number of piano students. Strains of Beethoven could be heard as they walked up the steps. Vashti reached up and pounded the beautifully polished brass knocker. There was a scramble of feet and the front door opened. Before them stood Amanda's younger brother, Alexander.

"Hello, Miss Smith. Hello, Professor Smith. Won't you please come in?"

Richard followed Vashti into the front foyer, taking off his hat as he entered. Amanda came out of the front parlor to their right. "Oh, Vashti, it is so good to see you!" They exchanged a quick hug. "Professor Smith, we will likely be busy all morning and part of the afternoon. My mother says to tell you that she will see to it that all of the band members will make it home properly escorted."

"Thank you, Amanda. I know that Vashti is in good company." Richard smiled, gave Vashti a peck on the cheek and tipped his hat as he turned to leave. As he walked down the steps he was very pleased to know the young women whom his daughter had chosen as friends. He thought it might be more accurate to say that the band had chosen them for each other, but it was a splendid group of young women.

"The other girls are here already, but we have just started to plan." Vashti followed Amanda into the parlor where Cybil, Sadie and Christina were seated. They exchanged warm greetings as Vashti and Amanda sat down. Amanda took the lead.

"I wrote to Bishop Beecher yesterday to inquire about Miss Blackthorne's funeral. I knew that Christ Church was the church where she attended services. I have here his reply:

My Dear Miss Fetkenheuer,

Thank you for your letter received this morning. I am currently in consultation with the Supervisor at Blackthorne Bunting Works to arrange for Miss Margaret Blackthorne's Memorial Service. We would be pleased to have the Betsy Ross All-Lady Silver Cornet Band participate.

We have chosen to do a Memorial service at the Founder's Hall on Saturday. So many from the community will want to attend that the supervisor, Mr. Hintz, thought that a public memorial followed by a private service at the grave site would be appropriate.

Would it be possible for the band to play a couple of marches to begin, then a solemn selection in the middle of the service and another march at the conclusion of the service?

I await your reply.

Yours,

Rev. Thadeus Beecher

After reading the letter Amanda looked up to see her friends' reactions. She could see they were determined to do this for Miss Blackthorne. "Do we agree to this arrangement?"

Heads nodded and bobbled along with a chorus of yeses. "We will need to call a rehearsal for tonight and perhaps a second one for Thursday as well. That is, if we can get the hall. I have plenty of postcards here. We have most all of the addresses and if we each write about ten cards we'll have this done in no time at all."

Christina chimed in, "I wonder if we could get an announcement into the evening edition of the newspaper. That way anyone who doesn't get a postcard by this afternoon would still be able to make it to the Thursday rehearsal. They will surely be running news of the memorial service."

"That's a wonderful idea," intoned Amanda. "I think my grandfather knows a reporter who can help us out. You start on the postcards and I'll see if grandfather is in between students."

They all started writing postcards. Amanda left the room, but was back quickly. "Grandfather had me write out an announcement about the rehearsal. We sent Alexander off to the Tribune with it. Hopefully he will make it in time for the evening edition."

It was quiet while they were busy writing. The room was filled with a sense of determination. In about a half an hour they were through. Amanda stacked them up and went off looking for another sibling to take them to the post office. Vashti broke the silence, "I think that Amanda should lead the band tonight. What do the rest of you think?" Sadie was dewy-eyed, but she bobbled her head "yes".

Cybil spoke up, "She is the logical person to lead us. Miss Blackthorne was always encouraging her and she is one of our very best musicians."

Just then, Amanda returned. Christina addressed her. "Amanda, we think you should lead the band tonight and for the memorial service as well. You are the obvious choice."

"Thank you, all. I had hoped to talk to you about this very thing. It is something that I would love to do to honor our dear teacher. Do you think the band will agree?"

Vashti was the next one to speak. "I'm quite sure my section will be pleased to have you lead us. Anyone who would be petty about this choice missed everything that Miss Blackthorne taught us about being professional in our work and supportive of one another."

"Well, then, let's talk about our repertoire. I think we must close with Mr. Sousa's *The Stars & Stripes Forever*. It was Miss Blackthorne's favorite march. I'm glad you got your piccolo fixed, Christina. You sounded wonderful last week at the cakewalk."

"Thank you, Amanda."

"You are welcome. Now I have an idea for our solemn piece. What do you think of playing George F. Root's *The Vacant Chair*? It is often played for bandsmen who have died and their chair is draped and set at the front of the stage. Maybe we could drape the podium with black crepe."

"I think that it's a lovely idea, but we don't have a band arrangement, do we?" Vashti looked concerned.

"We won't be able to rehearse it tonight, but we'll call that special rehearsal for Thursday evening if we can get the arrangement."

"I imagine that the Sons of Killarney Band might have it and they would probably let us borrow it," chirped Vashti.

"And I *imagine* that this might require a trip to the Conn store to see that nice Jack O'Brien," quipped Christina.

They all laughed.

"It's a great idea, Vashti. Let's pick our other two marches and then go down to the Conn store to ask. We need to do this efficiently with the rehearsal tonight and I'll want to study the parts as soon as possible." Amanda sat thoughtfully for a moment.

"Amanda, we can probably go to Christ Church as well. They aren't very far apart. Then you could talk to Bishop Beecher as well."

"That's a wonderful idea, Cybil! Well, let us choose our marches quickly and then we'll be off. What do you think of bringing out *Philadelphia Patriots* by Alessandro Liberati? We have played that recently and the band knows it well. Then we could play *The Banner March* by R.B. Hall to celebrate her founding of the Bunting Works. Miss Blackthorne would be proud to see us show our patriotism and I think it would be an excellent way to musically frame her life. Are we agreed?"

Yeses and bobbled heads made their approval.

"Then it is decided. Let me talk to Mother about going downtown to Conn and to Christ Church."

The other four girls were excited to be getting something accomplished. It was so much better than waiting. They were all of a similar mind that said doing was better than sitting.

Amanda returned. "Mother is ready to go with us. My grandmother will have a light soup luncheon ready for us when we come back. Have you all got you gloves and bonnets?"

Fastening on their obligatory hats and putting on their gloves, they met Mrs. Fetkenheuer in the front foyer. Out they went to the PRT station and the line that led to downtown Philadelphia. They decided to go to Christ Church first as Conn would be open and they could always leave a message with Jack or Daniel O'Toole about borrowing the band arrangement of *The Vacant Chair* if they didn't have a copy of it at Conn's. It was just a matter of minutes to their downtown stop. They weren't very chatty on the ride, each one lost in her thoughts. There was so much to do in such a short time.

The PRT stopped with a little jolt and they all stood up and popped out onto the platform and into the warmth of the sun. It was just a few blocks to Christ Church. Mrs. Fetkenheuer recommended that they stop at the Rectory next door to the church first. She thought that the Bishop would likely be there in his study. Sadie was Catholic and this was quite a new adventure to her. Christina and Amanda were Lutheran and Vashti and Cybil were Methodists.

At the Rectory door Amanda grasped the brass lion's head doorknocker and pounded. It gave a very pleasing, deep-throated thud, not unlike a 35-inch calfskin bass drum. You felt it more than heard it. After a short wait they heard soft footsteps. An elegant lady in a soft gray dress trimmed with a charming white lace collar opened the door. The hemline of her skirt was decorated with white ribbon appliquéd in large loops. Her lovely white hair was pulled back from her face and fastened in the back with a simple tortoise shell comb. She smiled warmly at the little ensemble and said, "Good morning ladies. I am Mrs. Beecher. Welcome to Bishop Beecher's residence. How may I help you?"

"Good Morning, Mrs. Beecher. I am Mrs. August Fetkenheuer. This is my daughter Amanda and these are her friends Cybil Hayes, Sadie Thomas, Christina Swenson and Vashti Smith. They are all members of the Betsy Ross All-Lady Silver Cornet Band. My daughter Amanda has been in communication with Bishop Beecher regarding Miss Blackthorne's memorial service. They have completed their plans for music and would like to leave a note for the Bishop regarding them."

Vashti marveled at the ease with which Mrs. Fetkenheuer spoke. She made a mental note to pay close attention to her manners. One day she would carry herself with that kind of grace and deportment.

"Oh, ladies, do come in! The Bishop is in his study, but I am certain that he will want to meet you. Come, come, our parlor is right here. Take a seat and I will go and speak with the Bishop."

All of the ladies entered the parlor and were seated on the lovely furniture. Vashti was admiring the twin pie-crust tea tables. Her mother had coached her to always observe rooms that she entered and to see if there were designs she might like in her own home one day. Mrs. Fetkenheuer spoke to the girls, " Ooh, those pie-crust tea tables could have been crafted by Thomas Afflick." She was seated in a Marlborough-leg armchair of mahogany with rich burgundy brocade upholstery. A pair of serpentine-front sofas provided a place where the others were seated. At that moment the Bishop and Mrs. Beecher entered the room. Mrs. Fetkenheuer stood and the others followed her lead. He was a tall man, very distinguished with gray hair that was white at the temples. He wore a black suit and a black shirt with a clerical collar.

"Good morning, ladies. What a distinct pleasure it is to meet you. You must be Mrs. Fetkenheuer," he said, taking her outstretched hand. She, in turn, introduced all of the band members ending with Amanda. "I am charmed to meet such lovely young ladies. Please, be seated." He took the matching Marlborough chair across from Vashti and his wife stood behind him to his left. "My wife tells me that you have made your plans for Miss Blackthorne's memorial service. Please, tell me about them."

Amanda was the one to talk for the band. She detailed the music, what they would wear and when their rehearsals were to take place.

"Will you be leading the band, Miss Fetkenheuer? I know that Miss Blackthorne would be proud to have you do it. She would sup with my wife and me at least twice a month and her conversation was often about her band members. She mentioned you often and was proud of all of you. I think I can speak for my wife as well when I say that I feel like I know each one of you."

They were surprised to hear this. None of them thought that she would have talked about them personally. Amanda found her voice. "I'll just start the band and then I'll be seated. We are a very well rehearsed group. The marches can be played without a conductor. If we can find an arrangement of *The Vacant Chair,* I may have to do some conducting, but I'll just stand by my place to lead."

"That's a fine idea. I am so pleased to have made your acquaintances. I know that the band will be splendid. Mrs. Beecher and I have attended many of your concerts. Unfortunately, we were not there on Friday. Thank you for taking the time to stop here and tell me of your plans."

With that they were dismissed. Each shook his hand and Mrs. Beecher led them to the door and wished them a good day. Back out in the sunlight they chatted about what a nice man Bishop Beecher seemed to be. They set their sights on C.G. Conn and decided to take the PRT as it was quite a number of blocks away and no proper lady should be seen in public with moisture on her brow.

On this ride the conversation centered on the décor of the rectory. Mrs. Fetkenheuer listened as the ladies discussed the styles and colors. She was delighted to hear their thoughts and to know that Amanda had such an interesting group of friends.

At their stop they left the PRT behind and walked the short block to the Conn store, revolving in through the shiny brass doors. The shop floor was busy, but Mr. Ritberger recognized the young ladies and excused himself for a moment, asking Jack to take over for him. Jack had flashed a wonderful smile at Vashti before he took Mr. Ritberger's place with confidence. At least, this is how Vashti chose to see him.

"How may I help you, ladies?"

"Hello Mr. Ritberger. I am Amanda Fetkenheuer. . . "

"You played the cornet solo last Friday evening at the cakewalk. It was wonderful!"

Amanda blushed charmingly. "Thank you, Mr. Ritberger. Actually we are here to see if you have a copy of George F. Root's *The Vacant Chair*. We want to perform it at Miss Blackthorne's Memorial Service on Saturday. If you don't have a copy we thought that Mr. O'Brien or Mr. O'Toole might be able to borrow it from the Sons of Killarney Band."

"I'll check on that right away." Looking around, he spied his shop clerk. "Um, Mrs. Tudor, would you please look through our band music inventory to see if we have *The Vacant Chair*?"

"Yes, Mr. Ritberger."

He continued talking to the ladies. "I see by the morning edition of the newspaper that the memorial service will be held on Saturday. I will certainly be there. In fact, I am closing the store on Saturday in her memory."

Mrs. Tudor returned. "There doesn't seem to be an arrangement of that selection, Mr. Ritberger."

"Thank you for looking." Turning to Amanda he said, "I'll send Mr. O'Brien over. Let me know if there is anything else I can do." Jack stepped over to talk with them giving each a warm smile and landing on the countenance of Vashti last and lingering on her sweet face. They both lit up in the other's company and this was not lost on the little ensemble.

Amanda interrupted their gazes, "Mr. O'Brien, we would like to borrow a piece of music from the Sons of Killarney Band. We think they may own an arrangement of George Root's *The Vacant Chair*." Amanda was going to be a wonderful leader, thought Vashti.

Jack smiled at her. "That's a wonderful idea, Miss Fetkenheuer. Let me just go back and ask Mr. O'Toole. I think he will know if it is in the band's library. I will be right back." He spun around and walked to the repair room with purpose. Striding up to Daniel's bench, he waited for him to finish adjusting a spring on a soprano saxophone and to acknowledge him. Daniel looked up at Jack and listened to his inquiry. Then Jack was off to the store.

"Mr. O'Toole says we have it. We'll make the necessary arrangements to get it. I can pick it up tomorrow evening before my dance lesson. May I deliver it to your home tomorrow evening, Miss Smith?"

Amanda would have liked to see the music earlier, but she would not stand in the way when the music from W.L. Cole's *Cupid's Arrow* waltz was playing around her two friends. All was arranged and the little ensemble revolved their way out of the Conn store into the sunshine and back to the PRT. They chatted about their very productive morning and were soon back at Amanda's house where her grandmother had readied for them a sumptuous luncheon of split pea soup with open-faced watercress and cream cheese sandwiches and iced tea.

The conversation was positively contrapuntal with each of the circle of friends sharing her thoughts of the day. The anticipation of a great performance gave them energy and resolve.

Soon after lunch the happy ensemble was on the PRT delivering each young musician to her home. Each made their farewell with a promise to be on time for that evening's rehearsal.

# Chapter 15

Amanda stood and held her hand up to silence the band. Her stomach was fluttery and her heart heavy as she started to take control of the band.

“Remember to sit up straight, ladies. You know this was important to Miss Blackthorne. We’ll start with the unison playing of our concert B-flat scale.”

She took the band through their warm-up routine and began with Liberati’s *Philadephia Patriots March.* This was one of the earliest pieces that the band had learned and it was one of their favorites in the repertoire. The rehearsal went well and all agreed to return for an additional rehearsal Thursday evening to learn their new piece.

As they were packing up, a man in a navy blue suit approached Amanda. “You are Miss Fetkenheuer, am I right?”

“Yes, I am.”

“I’m Harry Hintz, a longtime friend of the Blackthorne family. Margaret and I grew up next door to one another. I now manage the Blackthorne Bunting Works.”

“I’m pleased to meet you, Mr. Hintz,” she said extending her hand. The friends were now gathering around Amanda.

“Blackthorne Bunting Works will be taking care of the cost of the funeral and all of the arrangements. I think we’ll add more bunting to the stage. Margaret would have liked that. Bishop Beecher said that you have planned to drape the podium with black crepe. Do I understand that correctly?”

“Yes, we have. I hope that will be alright.”

"It's a wonderful gesture! I played snare drum in a boys' band many years ago and am familiar with this custom. Have you purchased the material yet?"

The ensemble exchanged glances. "I know we haven't made plans for that yet, Mr. Hintz."

"I know that many of these band members come from homes where an added expenditure would be difficult. May I suggest that Blackthorne Bunting Works provide this cloth and may we also provide black crepe armbands? I think most of the young ladies would know this is a proper sign of mourning. How about a lovely bouquet of calla lilies? The card on the bouquet will be signed from the band and no one other than us need ever know."

"That's very kind of you, Mr. Hintz. On behalf of the Betsy Ross All-Lady Silver Cornet Band, I accept."

"Excellent! Since you will have another rehearsal the armbands will be delivered here. I'll stop by again on Thursday just to see if anything else is needed. By the way, the band sounds wonderful. She would be so proud."

At that he wished the ensemble a good evening and walked out of the Founders Hall through the stage door and into the warm summer night. Stanley was waiting there with the Blackthorne Bunting Works carriage.

"Thank you, Stanley. We are through for the evening. Please, take me home. I am looking forward to seeing my family and having supper. It has been a long day. Please pick me up at 8:30 tomorrow morning."

"Yes, Mr. Hintz."

Vashti had one more thought to share with Amanda before leaving with Danforth. "Amanda, I have an idea. What about having the presentation cornet displayed on the podium Saturday? Jack could ask his father if we could have it back."

"That's a wonderful idea, Vashti! Yes, please ask Jack and we'll do just that, if it is possible."

# Chapter 16

The local newspapers were centered on writing tributes to Margaret Blackthorne. For the moment they would be kept busy interviewing those who knew her. There were many stories coming from people whom she had known over the years.

Many of her Blackthorne Bunting Works employees talked about how she helped them when they were just new immigrants to the United States. Her first stitchers were from all over Europe. Sometimes they did not speak English, so she would bring another stitcher along with her to translate when she hired new workers. Mothers with young children could work from home so they would still be able to supervise their families.

Sean looked at the articles. He was rubbing his chin and wondering why anyone would want to murder this lady. She didn't seem to have an enemy in the world. There wasn't a mean bone in her body. There just wasn't a single motive. And who could have gotten their hands on the arsenic? He had Brinkman out with a driver stopping to talk to all of the druggists in the district. He'd asked the Chief to send others out to investigate in their districts. So far nothing had turned up. Perhaps he could go over the notebooks again. He'd already done it twice.

No other names of people bad mouthing the band or Miss Blackthorne had turned up. He pondered this as he watched a fly crawl up the wall. Then a thought hit him. What if it was one of the members of the Betsy Ross All-Lady Silver Cornet Band? No. That wasn't possible. None of them had been alone with the cornet.

He'd talk to Jack again tonight. Maybe he would have an idea of some other way this could have happened at Conn. Maybe it was just an accident, intended for someone else. Sean was stumped.

♫

Henry Hintz met with the funeral parlor to make arrangements. The visitation would be held at Founder's Hall on Friday from noon until 7:00 p.m. The workers at Blackthorne Bunting Works would be given a half day off with pay. This would allow them to pay their respects as well.

Saturday would be the memorial service. Thousands were expected to attend. It was going to be an educated guess, but they did expect to fill up the hall. Margaret would be laid to rest in her band uniform. He had chosen a cypress wood coffin.

For the private interment on Sunday afternoon he had asked some of the ladies who were the top stitchers at Blackthorne Bunting Works to be the pallbearers. They would meet at the cemetery. The funeral home would see to it that Margaret's coffin was brought over in their hearse. Tradition had it that these ladies would wear white gloves. He had already ordered them and was expecting to have them on Friday morning when he would walk through the plant and hand them out.

Flowers were ordered. Extra bunting would be decorating the hall and would be hung Friday morning. He hand selected the men to do the work. They all had been with the company for many years. It was so unreal. Here he was planning the funeral for a childhood playmate. It still hadn't quite set in.

Jack was able to take his dance lesson and then drop over to the Sons of Killarney band rehearsal hall to pick up the band arrangement of *The Vacant Chair*. Daniel had sent word through the Irish community to say that Jack would be the courier. The rehearsal hall was actually the back of O'Shannon's Pub and that is where he now entered.

"Jack, me boy! Good ta see ya, lad. How's your Ma and Pa? I haven't seen them in a long time."

"They are doing well, Mr. O'Shannon, though Pop's working the Blackthorne case."

"Such a sad ting. She were a nice lady, that Miss Blackthorne. Well, here's your music, son. I know you've got ta get it delivered. Stop by again when ye can have a pint."

"Thanks, Mr. O'Shannon, I'll get this back when everything is over."

"The Sons of Killarney band is glad ta help out those lassies. Say hello to your parents."

"That I shall do."

Jack was back on the street. He decided to walk rather than take the PRT. He'd try to save the fare for another time. It was a beautiful night for a walk and he'd be able to see Vashti tonight. That made it extra special.

The Smith house was bright with light as he swung open the gate of the white picket fence and marched up the walk to the front porch steps. He could hear laughter coming from the parlor. This was always such a happy home to visit. The Smiths truly enjoyed one another's company. While they were all good conversationalists, they were also all very good listeners. They made a visitor feel like the most important person in the room. Bounding up the steps,he pounded the brass doorknocker and waited.

He heard footsteps and the door opened to reveal Danforth, who flashed him a big smile. "Hello, Jack! Won't you come it? May I take your hat?"

"Thanks, Danforth. Don't mind if I do."

Danforth took his striped-band skimmer and hung it on the hat rack in the foyer, pointing to the parlor as he did. All the Smiths turned to greet him. The Smith parlor was more formal than at his house, but there was a lot of love in that room and he always felt warmly welcomed and at ease.

"We're just playing charades, Jack. Looks like you got the music."

He strode over to Vashti and handed her the manila envelope that held the precious arrangement of *The Vacant Chair*. "Here it is, brought to you by carrier pigeon." Jack cooed and flapped his arms like wings.

Vashti was pleasantly caught off guard by his humor and she laughed full and long, as did the others. After regaining her composure she said, "Thank you, Mr. Pi-gee-on. May I ask another favor of you?"

"Certainly, Mademoiselle, and I shall endeavor to grant that favor before I fly the coop. Cooo!" Another arm flap ensued.

"Would you please ask your father if we could have Miss Blackthorne's presentation cornet back to display on the podium for the memorial service on Saturday? I know he may have to say no, but I'm just asking."

"That's a swell idea! I'll ask him this evening and I'll find a way to get it to the Founder's Hall before the memorial service on Saturday."

"Thank you so much. I know it would mean a lot to the band members."

With their business concluded the family regrouped for another game of charades. At the close, Jack thanked them for a lovely evening of entertainment and bid them goodbye. Skimmer on head, he skipped lightly down the steps, out the picket fence gate, closing it gently. He directed his feet to home, whistling the tune to *Hearts* by Charles K. Harris.

Once home he took his shoes off in the hallway leaving them for Seamus to polish. Opening the door, he spied his parents in the kitchen. The children must be asleep so he didn't call out a greeting to them, but walked into the kitchen and sat down. "Any news of the family?" His mother recounted a relatively calm day. "How's the investigation going, Pop?"

"Nothing new, son."

"That reminds me, Pop. Vashti asked if the band could have the presentation cornet back to put on display on the stage for the Memorial Service on Saturday. Is that possible?"

"Hmm. I'll have to check with the coroner." He paused for a bit, thinking. "We'll need to clean that mouthpiece up. Wouldn't want another death on our hands. One side of the bell is dented kind of flat. I think they will want to have that repaired. I'll see what I can do, Jack. This is a rather unusual circumstance, but I think Dr. Harrison will do everything possible to make it happen."

"I promised to get the cornet there in time for the memorial service, Pop."

"I'll get you an answer, Jack, and you can get it there and be their hero!" He smiled at his son. Jack had always been so focused on mechanical things that it was a delight to see his interest in Vashti Smith. She seemed like a lovely young lady.

# Chapter 17

Sean was out and about early. He was hopeful that today would bring about a break in the case. He probably had until Monday after the memorial service and burial before there was public outcry. Maybe some of the other precincts would report in with a lead. At the station he joshed with a handful of reporters. No need to cast a cloud over the investigation. Entering the station he swung through the gate toward his office. “Good morning, Evans.”

“Good morning, sir. Communications on your desk.”

“Thank you, Evans.” Sean took off his hat and coat, hung them on the coat tree and squeaked his chair up to his desk. While reading the memos, a shadow crossed his doorway. There was Brinkman. “Come in, Brinkman.” He smiled and indicated a seat. Brinkman closed the door, was seated and waited.

Sean finished the memos and there was nothing new. “Tell me that you have something for me, Adam.”

“I’m sorry, sir. I’ve come up empty. It’s maddening.”

“Well, we’ll keep digging. Do you have any new ideas to pursue?”

“I’d like to go back to Pick-Penn and interview all of the band members. Maybe there’s something there that we missed.”

“It’s worth a look. Take a driver and see what you can find.”

“Thank you, sir. I’ll do my best.” Brinkman stood and headed out of the office and through the lobby to the front door. He climbed into a wagon and sent the driver south again. Out of earshot he instructed the driver to head to Pick-Penn.

Meanwhile, back at the station, O’Brien had walked out to ask Evans to call the coroner’s office. “Switch it to my office when you get him.”

Back in his office, Sean sat down in his noisy chair and began to doodle. This was one of the ways that he thought. The telephone startled him back to reality and he picked up the machine, put the earpiece to his ear and spoke into the receiver. "O'Brien, here. Yes, Doc. The ladies in the Betsy Ross All-Lady Silver Cornet Band have requested to have Miss Blackthorne's presentation cornet to display at the memorial service on Saturday. Do you see any problem with that? I know it's a bit unusual." He sat listening. "Uhuh. Uhuh. We would have to clean the mouthpiece off. Okay. I'll tell them tonight and have someone pick it up from your office tomorrow during the day. That someone will probably be my son, Jack. He works for the Conn store. I think they will want to have the dent taken out of the bell. Have him sign it out just as we would anyone else. Thank you, Doc. Goodbye."

Sean hung up and doodled some more. He could hear the big clock ticking in the hall. He was hopeful that Brinkman would turn something up.

♫

Things at Conn had returned to relative normality. Jack spoke with Mr. Ritberger about getting the cornet repaired quickly the next day if he was able to get it from the coroner. Mr. Ritberger was only too happy to have the Conn New York Wonder cornet on display. He was thrilled to have Conn prominently represented at the memorial. While he liked Miss Blackthorne, her passing was likely to put a dent in his business. Any advertising would certainly help.

Brinkman arrived at Pick-Penn and was ushered into Mr. Kitridge's office. Mr. Young greeted him. "Welcome back to Pick-Penn Coal & Smelting, Patrolman Brinkman. How may I be of service to you today?"

"I'd like to interview all of the company bandsmen. Would that be possible?"

"Please, have a seat and I will work out the arrangements with Mr. Kitridge." With that he knocked on the office door and entered. After a few minutes he returned. "We have our boardroom available for your use. If you will follow me, it is just through this door."

Mr. Young opened the door to an oak paneled room with a long oak table and twenty chairs. There was beautiful artwork on the walls including oil portraits of the founders Robert Pickwick and Andrew Penn.

"I'll have the band members brought up and sent to you. Let me know if there is anything that you need."

"Thank you, Mr. Young."

♫

Vashti was practicing her horn. She wanted to be at her very best for the memorial service and she was of the opinion that she could help lead tonight by honing her horn part in advance.

She hoped that the band members wouldn't be overcome by emotion at the service. Sadie was so tenderhearted, but she would likely memorize her parts as she had done for *Rough Riders* march. Christina would do well and so would Amanda. She hadn't looked to see if there was a snare drum part or if the percussion was *tacet.* Either way Cybil would be strong on her part.

Vashti found herself tracing the lace in the curtains and resolved to go downstairs to the front parlor. Maybe she would do some embroidery or she could always read. She had just begun Nathaniel Hawthorne's The House of Seven Gables, and Mother was very likely downstairs. She would always have an interesting topic to discuss. It would be a good way to use her time before supper and then the evening rehearsal.

# Chapter 18

"Danforth, I'm ready to go!" Vashti hollered upstairs.

"Vashti, don't yell." Her mother was always coaching. "It isn't proper."

"I'm sorry, Mother. I'll try to do better." They were both smiling. Danforth appeared and offered to carry Vashti's French horn.

"Why, thank you, dear brother of mine."

"Have a good rehearsal, Vashti, and enjoy your billiards, Danforth. Oh, you have your music for the band, yes?"

"Thank you, Mother," they chimed in unison as they went out the front door. As they were walking toward the PRT, they chatted. "Jack O'Brien is coming over to the Founders Hall tonight to tell me if we can get the presentation cornet for the memorial service on Saturday."

"You seem to have taken a shine to Jack. He's a good fella. Comes from a good family. Has a good job with a bright future at Conn."

"Danforth, have you been asking around regarding Jack?"

"Maybe just a little," he said smiling at his sister. "You are my little sister and I care about you. I wouldn't want you getting attached to the wrong sort of man."

"That is very sweet of you, Danforth. I do think that I could allow my head to be turned by Jack O'Brien." They had arrived at their PRT stop just as the car rolled up. Other band members were already on board with their chaperones and the conversation changed to greetings and general news.

When they got off their car, Danforth carried Vashti's French horn into the backstage area. He bid her good evening and went to engage in a few friendly games of billiards with a promise to be back later. Vashti had the borrowed band arrangement in a little carrying bag. She said goodbye to Danforth and went in search of Amanda.

"Amanda! How nice to see you this evening. I have the band arrangement for you."

Christina was across the podium from Amanda. She motioned to the bag and she chirped, "I *imagine* that you enjoyed that part of the planning." They all smiled.

Amanda, who was looking through the parts, spoke up. "How about splitting the parts up by sections and handing this out? I think we will be able to work this through very nicely this evening." The music was all in order so she handed the piccolo part and all of the clarinet parts to Christina. Vashti got the horn and saxophone parts and so forth until all the parts had been distributed to the band members. Rehearsal began and they read through the new selection with coaching from Amanda. The other selections were practiced as well and by the end of the rehearsal each band member knew her part well. Amanda announced the meeting time for Saturday and wished all of the members a good evening.

The ladies were busy packing up their instruments and saying their goodbyes. Amanda was at the front of the stage answering last minute questions. "The ladies were already looking to her for leadership," thought Vashti. "Maybe they would be able to continue the band after all." There were questions to be answered like where they would rehearse and how they would purchase new music and instruments and uniforms for new members they might recruit. But first they would need to display themselves well to honor the memory of Miss Blackthorne.

Amanda smiled at Mr. Hintz as he walked to her side. "The band sounds very nice, Miss Fetkenheuer. I know that Margaret would be so proud of you and all of these young women. Thank you for your fine work."

“That is very kind of you, Mr. Hintz. I am honored to be able to lead the band for this and I think I can speak for all of the members when I say we are so pleased to be included in the memorial service.”

“Is there anything else you will need between now and Saturday? I know that the black armbands will be delivered here tomorrow. I’ve asked that they be set up back stage. I heard you announce to the band that they would be wearing them. Will you be able to show them how to wear them or should I have someone here to help with that?”

“I think it would help to have someone here for that purpose. That will be one less thing for me to think about.”

“Of course. I’ll have a few ladies from Blackthorne Bunting here to assist. They will be only too happy to help out. I’ll be here for the visitation tomorrow and also will be here early on Saturday. Do not hesitate to call on me for anything. I want this to be a very special service for all involved. Margaret was like a sister to me.”

“Thank you, Mr. Hintz. I appreciate all you have done for the band.”

“I see that your brother is here to escort you home. I won’t keep you any longer. Have a good evening.”

“Good night, Mr. Hintz.”

He walked out of the hall and saw Stanley at the carriage waiting for him. “Home, Stanley. We will have several long days ahead of us. We might as well get some rest.”

“Yes, Mr. Hintz.” He closed the carriage door, climbed to the drivers seat, and called to the bays, “Get up now!” The blue carriage rolled off into the night.

♫

Vashti and Danforth were stepping off the PRT on the way home. He knew his sister well enough to know that she was off in her own thoughts. “Hello, Vashti. Where are you?” he said in a dreamy tone.

“Oh, I’m just thinking about the next few days and wondering what will happen to the band after Saturday. It’s such a wonderful group of musicians and I’ve made some very close friends through this band. It seems such a shame to have that all disappear in three days. I think we’ll try to keep the band going, but there are so many things we’ll need to decide on. We may need a new place to rehearse, as I’m quite certain that we won’t be able to afford the Founders Hall. Miss Blackthorne paid for the rental of the hall. I should probably not think about this now, but, Danny, I love playing in the band. I don’t want to lose both Miss Blackthorne and the band in such a short period of time.” She looked up at him with her brow furrowed.

“I am afraid that I have no answers for that, Vashti, but I think the way that you and the others have worked to make the music for the memorial service happen bodes well for the future. Amanda is a great leader for the group.”

“Well, that is what is weighing heavy on my mind this evening. I also don’t know if we’ll get the cornet for Saturday and we might not know until then if it will work.”

“Vashti, you know Jack very well. If there is any way to bring it about, Jack is the man to do it.” She smiled at her brother and they walked the last few blocks in silence. Friday would be a big day.

♫

At the O’Brien home supper had been consumed and evening was winding down as the younger children went to bed. Sean was then able to talk to his son. “I spoke with Doc Harrison today. He’s the coroner. He'll have the cornet cleaned up and ready for you tomorrow. I told him you would drop by and pick it up. Do you think that will be possible?"

"I spoke to Mr. Ritberger about getting it repaired today. He was happy to take care of that and Mr. Stein knows that it will be coming. He will fit it into his repair schedule tomorrow. Pop, I know this is crazy, but I think that one of the band members ought to be involved in this. They worked so hard to give that cornet to Miss Blackthorne and were so good about keeping it a secret and it is an expensive instrument. They have an emotional and financial investment in this."

"What are you suggesting, Jack?"

"I would like to have Vashti come along to pick it up, but I don't know if that would be improper. I don't know how to get notice to her before the visitation tomorrow. The Smiths don't have a telephone."

Sean rubbed his chin thinking. "How about this? I'll take a police wagon over to the Smith house in the morning. If it is all right with her father I'll bring her to the Conn store where we will pick you up and then go to the coroner's office to pick up the cornet. I'll go in first to see to it that everything will be appropriate for a young lady to enter. Then we'll loop back to Conn where the repair can be made and you may continue working. Miss Smith will be dropped off back at her home with the cornet in hand to be taken to the hall on Saturday by the Smith family. Will that help you to play the hero, my son?"

"Pop, that would be swell!"

"Then that is how we'll work it out. I'll be able to stay in touch with the station if anything else comes up. We'll have extra patrolmen out for the visitation tomorrow anyway. No one knows how many people will show up for this. Could be quite a large number. We're not expecting any trouble, but it won't hurt to have a police presence there just in case."

“Thanks, Pop. I think the band members will be so thrilled to have the presentation cornet there.”

“Off to bed, Jack. We all have a long weekend ahead.”

# Chapter 19

Friday dawned sunny and warm. Sean was out the door early again. He'd have some extra work with driving around the city, but it was far better than sitting in his office trying to run through all of the notes again. Brinkman would be in with his notes on the bandsmen from Pick-Penn. He was hopeful that something might be found there.

There were no reporters on the steps so far today. That was a relief. Entering the station the lobby area was empty as well. "Good morning, Evans."

"Good morning, sir."

Entering his office he found Brinkman already there paging through a notebook. He liked the way this young man worked. Efficient, on time and polite, he was already a fine policeman. "Good morning, Adam. I hope you are well this morning and I furthermore hope that you have something for me."

"Good morning, sir. I interviewed every one of the bandsmen at Pick-Penn. If there is anyone there with a motive for killing Miss Blackthorne, I don't know who it would be. I think that the stories about Casswell griping about the ladies band just stem from a fella who was trying to talk big around his friends. No one there seems to have taken him very seriously. I have all the names of the players and notes from each person. I've looked to see if any of the stories are the same as if they memorized something. It just doesn't exist. I have two notebooks here for you to look over." He looked at Sean with tired eyes.

"Well, son, thank you for trying that approach. Leave the notebooks here and I'll have a look later in the day. I'll need to do some running around this morning. Check with Evans to see if there is some deskwork to do. It will do you good to work on something else for a while."

"Will do," he said, standing and walking out of the office.

Sean paged through the notebooks skimming over Brinkman's neat penmanship. It all appeared to be quite organized and thorough. He'd have to look these over later. Right now he thought he'd better get to the task at hand and get that cornet over to Conn. Grabbing his hat and coat, he strode out of his office, through the swinging doors and to the front door, calling over his shoulder, "I'll be out most of the morning, Evans. If you need to contact me, try the Coroner's office or the Conn store. I'll check in."

There were a couple of official police wagons at the curbside. He chose the nicest conveyance, a carriage, since he'd have Miss Smith with him. She would be more comfortable and he didn't wish to give the impression that she was being brought in for questioning. It was inevitable that some tongues would wag with gossip. He'd do his best to keep that to a minimum. First he'd pick up Jack at Conn. Then they'd go to the Smith's and request to have Miss Smith come with them. He was building a route in his head as the driver took him to the band instrument store.

♫

The first thing that Jack did when he arrived at work was to talk to Mr. Ritberger about the day. He thought that there would be no problem with his being out and about on the cornet run, but he thought it best to ask permission right away.

For his part, Arthur Ritberger was happily supportive of Jack. He had rarely had as fine a young employee as Jack. Daniel had spoken very highly of him and Jack had lived up to that recommendation and then some. He could not remember a time when he was late and he also knew that he wasn't standing at the door ready to run out at the end of the day. Someday he would likely take over Daniel's bench as the woodwind repairman. He could happily condone the morning trip to fetch the presentation cornet.

Not long after the revolving door was unlocked, Sgt. O'Brien spun into the store.

"Good morning, Mr. Ritberger. I have come to gather up my son, if that is alright with you."

"Good morning, Sergeant O'Brien. Jack has already spoken to me and we'll be able to muddle along without him for the morning," he said with a warm smile. "Bruno Stein is our brass man. He is ready to make the repair to the cornet as soon as it comes into the store. He'll have you on your way in plenty of time."

Jack had come into the store carrying his hat. He looked at Sean and they nodded and were revolving their way out the door. It was a short ride over to the Smith house. Father and son alighted from the carriage and approached the door. Sean banged the brass doorknocker and waited. The door was opened by Hettie who was somewhat taken aback by the police officer at the door.

"May I help you, sirs?"

"We've come to speak with Professor Smith. Is he at home?"

"Certainly. Do come in." She moved aside, they both removed their hats and stepped into the foyer. Hettie knocked lightly on the study door and a muffled voice was heard from inside. She opened the door and said, "There's Jack O'Brien and his father here to see you, Professor." They could hear a little rustle from the study and Richard Smith appeared in hallway.

"Thank you, Hettie." She took one last look at the two men and scuttled her way to the kitchen. "Good morning. How may I help you this morning?"

"Please, pardon our unannounced intrusion. We are endeavoring to get the presentation cornet to Miss Blackthorne's memorial service tomorrow. My son Jack suggested to me last evening that we come by your home and invite Miss Vashti to come along with us and eventually return here with the cornet. We'll be going to the coroner's office to pick it up. I will personally make sure that there is nothing there that a young lady should not see. You or Mrs. Smith may certainly come along." He waited while Richard processed the request.

"I don't see why she shouldn't go with you. I believe she and my wife are in the parlor. We can continue our conversation there." He led the way into the sunny room and did indeed find the two ladies there doing needlework.

"My dear, the O'Brien's have come to request that Vashti accompany them to pick up the presentation cornet for tomorrow's memorial service. It's a little unusual, but I think it would be good for our daughter to be out and about this morning. Would you like to do this, Vashti?"

"Yes, Father!" She was a little too enthusiastic and just smiled at him.

"I think I will go along with you. Well, daughter, get your hat and gloves."

In a matter of moments they were all gathered at the front door and soon out in the morning sun. The conversation was light and mostly about trivial things like the weather. Vashti and her father learned that the next stop was the coroner's office.

At police headquarters they climbed up a vast number of steps to the main entryway. This was a serious building of solemn red brick. Upon entering one noticed immediately how the echo of footsteps rolled about the inner corridor. After holding the door first for Vashti and then her father and Jack, Sean followed them into the space. "We'll go to our left. Dr. Harrison's office is there."

The second office to the left had a door with a frosted window and a nameplate:

Dr. Mortimer Harrison, Coroner

Sean turned the doorknob and entered. There was a counter in the front of the office where two clerk's looked up from their desks.

Doc Harrison was in a glassed office at the back. One of the clerks was rising to greet the quartet when the doctor stepped out of his office and said, "I'll take care of these people, Mike." He extended his hand to Sean, who shook it and introduced the entourage beginning with Vashti.

"Good morning. We have an evidence holding room in this office for current cases. I brought the cornet up here Monday morning. Please come back with me. It's on a table in the room." They followed him behind the counter and to a large room on the right where the door was standing open. There on the table stood the cornet case. Behind it was the single rose found at Miss Blackthorne's head. It was withered and the bright red was now dark and almost black.

Doc Harrison opened the case for them to see the cornet with its dented bell. Jack looked at it closely, but did not touch it. He looked to Vashti and said, "I think Mr. Stein will be able to take that dent out and make her look new again." Vashti smiled. She hadn't seen the cornet since the cakewalk and was concerned about its condition.

"I have cleaned the mouthpiece off, but I would suggest that no one play on it just to be safe." He took the mouthpiece out as he was talking. Vashti furrowed her brow and cocked her head to one side, but listened intently. Sean noticed her motion and made a mental note of it.

When Doc Harrison had finished his spiel, he brought out an evidence release form. "Which one of you will sign for the cornet?"

"I'll take responsibility for it, Dr. Harrison." Richard stepped forward, took the fountain pen and signed his John Hancock to the form. After some polite banter, they shook hands. Jack laid the cornet in its case and the quartet headed back to the carriage. Once they were settled into their seats Sgt. O'Brien looked at Vashti and asked, "What was troubling you about the cornet mouthpiece?"

"I'm not sure, but I don't think that is the right mouthpiece. I thought that we asked for a Benjamin Bent mouthpiece. Amanda told us that is the kind that Miss Blackthorne played." Pointing toward the black case she said, "That's a different mouthpiece in there."

Jack was about to open the case when his father stopped him. "Wait until we get back to the store, Jack. We'll look at it there." They sat in silence all the way back to the store. When they revolved their way into the store, Mr. Ritberger was about to greet them when he noticed the serious look on everyone's face. O'Brien spoke, "May we use your office, Mr. Ritberger? You should come with us."

"Certainly," he replied leading the way. They all paraded down the walkway and up the three steps into the office. Jack took the case over to the round table and set it down unlatching the cover and opening it up. He took the mouthpiece out and held it out to Vashti who read, "Wonder Model 19." Jack looked at his father. "That's the wrong mouthpiece, Pop." They all looked toward Mr. Ritberger. "It can't be! I checked it myself. It should be a Benjamin Bent model."

O'Brien took over. "Let me see it Jack," he said, holding out his hand. Jack set it in the palm of his father's hand. Sean then took it over to Mr. Ritberger so he could see for himself. "Oh, my! That isn't the mouthpiece that was in there when it left the store! I cleaned a Benjamin Bent mouthpiece and placed it in the case myself." He was shaking and wide-eyed, trying to make Sean understand.

"Take a deep breath, Mr. Ritberger. No one is making any accusations. Let's just confirm that this is not the mouthpiece that was ordered. Is that correct?"

"That is true." He was obviously distressed.

"The first thing is to get the cornet fixed for tomorrow's memorial service. Jack, would you please take it back to Mr. Stein. Put the mouthpiece back and give it to him to fix. Ask how long it will take and then come back here."

Jack took the mouthpiece from his father's hand, replaced it in the case, closed it and took it to the repair shop.

"Let's all just calm down a bit. Mr. Ritberger, I am making no accusations here. We know that that isn't the same mouthpiece. I believe you when you say you put the other mouthpiece in the case. Please, just relax. Let me think for a moment."

They all stood in the office staring at the Oriental rug. The clock on the wall seemed thunderously loud. No one spoke and Sean rubbed his chin. Jack returned. "Bruno said he would have it done in about ten minutes. He can put the bell back into round and then tap the dent out on a mandrel. The metal wasn't actually stressed so it will look brand new again." He realized that no one was really paying attention to him so he just stood there and let the clock tick.

Sean broke the silence. "With the visitation this afternoon and the store being closed tomorrow, I just want to get the cornet into Professor Smith's hands. I'm going to review the interview notes when I get back to the station. I want you all to keep this new information to yourselves. Am I understood?" They all nodded. "Jack, please, check on Mr. Stein and bring the cornet back here when he is done." Jack left the office again.

"When he brings the cornet back, I will accompany the Smiths back to their home and then I'll be back at the station. Mr. Ritberger, call me there if you notice anything unusual here like your workers acting suspiciously."

Jack returned to the office with the cornet. He was about to hand it to Professor Smith when his father intervened, "Set it on the table again, Jack." Jack complied and Sean walked over to open the case again. He took the mouthpiece out and inspected it. It was still a Wonder Model 19. He replaced the mouthpiece, closed and latched the case and handed it to Professor Smith. "Let's be about our day." He led the way for the Smiths walking through the store and revolving out the door to the waiting carriage. He instructed the driver to return to the Smith home. There was no conversation. They all knew that something important had happened, but no one really knew what it might be.

At the Smith home he climbed out of the carriage and offered his hand to Vashti as she stepped down. "Sergeant O'Brien, do you think this could be important to the case?" She looked at him hopefully.

"It's new information, Miss Smith. Sometimes these things can help us out. Do not worry about it too much. You will have much to think about with the memorial service tomorrow afternoon."

"Good day, Sgt. O'Brien."

"Good day to you, Professor Smith, and to you, Miss Smith." He tipped his hat and climbed back into the carriage. The driver shook the reigns and they were off to the station. Sean sat there rubbing his chin. It was new information, but what could it mean? He'd been there for those interviews. In all of his years of police work he had developed a nose for detecting liars. He didn't think any of those people were involved, but how on earth could that mouthpiece have been switched?

Back at the station he burst into the foyer and bellowed, "Evans, get Brinkman up here on the double."

"Yes, sir!" He got up from his desk and went to back of the station where Brinkman was working in booking. "Sgt. O'Brien is back and he is steamed. He wants you up there on the double." Adam was out from behind the desk and up to Sean's office in a jiffy.

"You wanted me, sir?"

"Come in and close the door." Brinkman complied and then sat when O'Brien motioned for him to do so.

"I've just come from the Conn store and the coroner's office. Vashti Smith noticed that the mouthpiece in the case was not what it was intended to be. I want to go over the interviews to see if there are any discrepancies. Here's the notebook with the Conn interviews. Read them aloud to me." Sean had learned this technique from an old beat cop who told him it always sounded more true to life when read aloud.

When Adam finished reading, he looked up at Sean. "Do you notice any inconsistencies, Adam?"

"I don't think so, sir. These are all just narrations of their days. Nothing seems out of order or contrived. By the time you were there asking questions, they would all have known about Miss Blackthorne's death. If one of them thought we were on to them, they would have looked guilty."

"I agree. Now I have to do this, Adam. I was not there for the interviews at the Smith house. Take up the second notebook and read those aloud."

Adam knew that Sean was just double-checking his interview tactics. He felt that he had done an exemplary job of interviewing the Smiths and he always tried to make clear notes. Having exchanged the notebooks he began reading aloud once again. When he looked up at Sean at the end the older man was looking out the window and rubbing his chin. It was quiet for a few minutes.

"I don't hear anything unusual in those either. Now, Adam, think for just a moment. Is it possible that you could have been swayed by a pretty girl and wrote down anything that would lean in her favor?"

Adam realized what the older man was asking. He thought for a moment and replied, "I think that I wrote everything down in a true and clear manner."

"Thank you, Adam. I don't think she is a murderer either, but I wouldn't be doing my job if I didn't ask. Hmm. Best that you go back to the work that you were doing and cogitate on this new bit of information."

Adam stood up, put the notebook back on O'Brien's desk and went back to booking, leaving the office door open. His head was spinning with this new piece of information, but he didn't have any answers.

# Chapter 20

Vashti was dressed in her black crepe dress for the visitation. It was appropriate for funerals and she and her mother had both felt that black would be the proper dress. They were intending to go to the Founder's Hall at about 3:00 thinking that the crowd would be larger at the beginning and then again at the end.

The entire Smith family would go to pay their respects together. So they met in the front foyer, as was their custom when traveling to events as a family. Mrs. Smith checked over the clothing of each of her children and her husband, too. She always wanted them to look their best in public.

It was a beautiful summer's day as they walked together to the PRT. The visitation was a solemn event, so they were not very chatty as they walked. As they got on the PRT, they nodded to friends who were also in black crepe to honor Miss Blackthorne. Vashti was amazed to see the number of people wearing black and traveling with such serious demeanors.

Soon they were at their stop where her father helped her mother out of the car and Danforth offered her his arm so she would not catch her foot on the gap as she stepped out. Looking ahead they could see a line of people outside of the Founder's Hall. Vashti whispered to Danforth, "There must be two hundred people in that line."

"And think how many more inside of the building and it's still early in the day."

The Smith family joined the line. Her father shook hands with a few of the men he knew and her mother nodded to several whom she knew as well. Vashti could see a few band members and their families and she nodded her "hello" mimicking her mother. The line moved along rather quickly as the funeral directors wanted to be able to get everyone to file past the casket. So far all was working well.

Inside the building you could hear the shuffle of feet and Vashti remembered that Miss Blackthorne had pronounced it an acoustically perfect place to rehearse a band. She wondered about the future of the band and she found herself becoming a bit emotional about the possibility that the band would never play in this magnificent space again. She was already feeling teary about the loss of Miss Blackthorne and seeing her in her band uniform for the last time.

She could see the open casket now. People were walking by slowly and a few stopped to cross themselves and to say a prayer. She could hear some of the women sniffling and thought immediately of Sadie. Without craning her neck she looked around to see if Sadie was near, but she didn't see her.

The front of the stage was lined with huge flower bouquets. There was a spray of dahlias across the coffin. The bouquet closest to Miss Blackthrone's feet had a large blue ribbon that had the words "Dear Teacher" in white painted on it. Vashti thought this must be the flower arrangement from the band that Mr. Hintz had told her and the other band ladies that he would have delivered. It was stunningly beautiful. The hall had the sweet scent of just cut flowers. Every one of the flower arrangements was beautiful. It was a sight to behold.

The Smiths walked past the coffin and paid their last respects to Miss Blackthorne. Richard and Elisabeth watched Vashti out of the corner of their eyes to see that she did well. All of the parents of the band ladies were concerned about the future of music for their daughters. On top of the loss of a dear teacher and friend, they hoped that the young ladies would be able to continue to develop their unique musical skills.

Once past the casket they followed the corded off aisle out of the building. No one really stood and chatted. It wasn't the happy atmosphere that surrounded the musicians and audience after one of their concerts. The Smith family returned to their homes via the PRT. They were all subdued and spent the remainder of the afternoon until supper doing various projects, alone with their own thoughts.

At supper the conversation was relaxed, but no one was particularly jolly. They enjoyed a first course of consome soup with olives and celery on the side. Then came cold roast pig with escaloped oysters and Vienna rolls with honey. For desert this evening there was a lovely brick cheese with candied walnuts. Thus fortified, the conversation turned to the next day.

"What time will you need to be at the Founder's Hall tomorrow, Vashti?" asked her father, sliding his chair back from the table just a tad.

"I am to do my warm-up here at home and then be at the Founder's Hall by 12:30 p.m. We will enter silently to the stage. Amanda will seat the band and she will start our first march. I believe that Bishop Beecher will actually start the service. I think I should actually be there a bit before that as we'll need to get our black crepe arm bands on."

He nodded to himself and steepled his hands together in front of his chest. This was a sign that he was thinking. "I think it would be respectful to Miss Blackthorne if we did not engage in any games this evening. I think I will go to my study and read a bit."

In short order the family had scattered to various points of the house.

# Chapter 21

Vashti's excitement was palpable as she entered the stage door. Danforth carried her French horn backstage and then hurried out to join his family. There was a huge crowd headed into the hall and he didn't want to lose his seat. The Smith family had developed the habit of sitting in the same general area for each concert. They could see their daughter and she knew where to look for them.

When the band was first started, Miss Blackthorne had spoken poetically of the joy their daughters would experience knowing that their families were there to support them. Concerts by the Betsy Ross All-Lady Silver Cornet Band were always free and entire families were encouraged to attend. She said that it was good for young children to be exposed to great music. The families were out in full force today. Indeed, it seemed like the whole city was on its way to the memorial service.

Backstage the musicians were getting their black crepe armbands in place. Instruments were put together, but the usual din was missing as each player had executed her warm-up at home. Amanda was walking around greeting the players and she smiled as she approached Vashti. "Your young man has triumphed, Vashti. The presentation cornet is out on the podium with a single red rose. Very nice."

Vashti smiled warmly. It was a thrill to think that Jack had come through with flying colors. Everything was coming together nicely like a well rehearsed Franz von Suppe overture. Fifteen minutes before the memorial service was to begin, the band members began to line up to go onstage. They were resplendent in their uniforms. Each had taken particular care to see that her instrument was polished. All the ladies were ready to perform an outstanding tribute and farewell to their dear teacher.

At Amanda's signal, they filed on stage. The soft din of voices slowly quieted in the hall. Bishop Beecher entered and sat down in an ornate chair on the floor below the stage to the right, but still in view of everyone in the hall. He was a tall man and his impeccably pressed black robes were imposing.

Amanda stood up and started the band in Alessandro Liberati's *Philadelphia Patriots*. The pulse was even and lively just as they had been taught. The percussion was crisp and well-balanced. The audience could feel the bass drum more than hear it. It was as if the beat caused their hearts to all beat along in time with the band.

When the band finished, it was quiet for a moment and then Bishop Beecher started to clap. The whole crowd joined in loudly and enthusiastically. Vashti was thankful for the Bishop starting the applause. Since this was like a church service, she was certain that the audience members would never have clapped in church. He had remedied an awkward situation.

Amanda stood up again as the applause died down. With a clear preparatory beat, the band took a breath and was cleanly into R.B. Hall's *The Banner*. The tuning was exceptional today. You could tell that every one of the band members was determined to play her very best to honor Miss Blackthorne. Vashti had sneaked a quick peek at Sadie in-between pieces. Sure enough, she had tears running down her cheeks, but the tuba section was strong. They had that beautiful lift that was a characteristic of a well-played march. It was difficult to execute, but Miss Blackthorne had worked painstakingly on this style in rehearsal, continually admonishing each young musician to make music and not just play notes.

The band ended with a full, in-tune stinger, as they called the last note, and the assembly burst into applause. After an appropriate time, Bishop Beecher stood, walked up on stage and over to the podium. "No doubt most of us in this hall have never been to a memorial service that began with two artistically played marches. It is certainly a first for me. But while we are here to mourn the loss of a dear friend, teacher, employer and pillar of the community, we also want to celebrate her life. A life that was filled with band music."

The Bishop went on to detail much of Margaret Blackthorne's life. He talked of her tenacity in starting Blackthorne Bunting Works and admonished all to strive for this kind of dedication in their work.

Vashti was watching the audience. Many were drying tears. She felt a little teary herself, but reminded herself that the band was due to play again soon and that she needed to maintain her composure.

She heard Bishop Beecher talking about the Betsy Ross All-Lady Silver Cornet Band.

"Margaret Blackthorne believed in the power of music to help these young ladies in their lives. While we have enjoyed the music that they have performed today, it is really so much more than a march or two that is on display. She taught all of these young ladies the discipline that it takes to practice small sections of pieces until they are perfected. Hours and hours of practice that some of you parents have listened to for years now.

Perhaps you can hear your daughter's part as she plays in the band and now you also hear the other parts and how the whole composition comes together. These young musicians have learned that there are no unimportant notes. She hoped that they would all learn that they had roles to play in life, too. Each and every one of them is important to the composition. She felt that a ladies band was an excellent way to bring out the best in each young lady."

Vashti was using her eyes to look around at the other band members. She, and all the other musicians, had been taught to sit still to avoid drawing attention to herself, but she could see tear stained cheeks. She imagined that they were all hoping that some way could be found for the band to continue. That would be the best and most lasting tribute to Miss Blackthorne. Amanda was standing and Vashti realized that it was time for them to play their solemn selection, *The Vacant Chair*.

When they finished the piece, Vashti could hear people crying in the hall. A sniffle came from the back of the band and she knew it was

Sadie. She was trying to keep her composure because they were not done playing yet, but it was difficult.

Bishop Beecher walked to the stage where he thanked the hundreds of people who had worked so hard to honor Miss Blackthorne. He reminded the assembly that this was a rather unusual event in that marches weren't usually at played at times of great sorrow, but this memorial service was a celebration of their dear friend's life and that this was also a celebration of her new life in heaven.

"In a moment I will pronounce the benediction and then the band will play their final selection, *The Stars & Stripes Forever*, Margaret's favorite march. Following that musical postlude you will be free to leave the hall and let your hearts be light."

He stood in the center of the stage, raised his hands over the assembly and pronounced the benediction. Vashti listened to his strong voice as it carried through the hall. When he was done, Amanda stood and brought her right hand up to start the band. All of the instruments came up and the percussion had their sticks at the ready. A precise upbeat and the band played the introduction. Their sound was strong. The first strain was played in an impeccable scherzo style. The second strain was played lyrically in contrast with beautifully shaped phrases, *forte* the second time through. Then they made the transition to the new key of the trio section, adding the requisite flat. They performed this section like a grand opera aria, each musician playing her part with great emotion. The low brass and woodwinds were thrilling when they brought in the dogfight strain and the upper brass and woodwinds were equal to the task in their replies.

Then Christina played the piccolo solo. She had performed this solo flawlessly hundreds of times, but it had a little something extra today. A repeat to the dogfight strain brought a slight change in tone quality. Just a bit of snarl as Miss Blackthorne had taught them. The chromatic passages were setting the audience up for the final strain, when Amanda, still seated, shot her hand up to give the band an ever so slight *ritardando* before sailing into the *Grandioso*.

Amanda was piccoloing, the trombones sliding and the cornets corneting with the entire band supporting them. The assembly began to clap along on the beat. Vashti knew the band members were outdoing themselves. It was amazing to be in the center of this sound and then suddenly the assembly was standing and applauding wildly, tears stained many cheeks and some were waving their handkerchiefs in the air.

Amanda stood the band up and they could hear cheers from the audience. They stood for a short while and then she pointed for them to leave the stage. Backstage they gathered in small groups hugging one another and assuring each other that they had done their best performance ever and that Miss Blackthorne would have been so proud of them.

Vashti sought out her group of friends. She hugged tenderhearted Sadie as they gathered. When Amanda joined the little group, Vashti spoke up, “Amanda, I’ve been thinking. We should have the band members vote at the next rehearsal about what they want done with the presentation cornet. I know it’s soon, but it’s important.”

“That’s a great idea Vashti,” said Cybil. “I think you should take it home with you for safekeeping.”

They all agreed. Vashti tugged Sadie’s sleeve, “Sadie, come with me to see if it is okay for me to take the cornet and the case.” The two band members walked out to the front of the stage. There was Bishop Beecher shaking hands and talking softly with what looked to be members of his church. Mr. Hintz was near to the Bishop, but closer to the closed coffin. He was speaking with people who looked like they might be employees of Blackthorne Bunting Works. Though composed, he would dab a tear from the corner of his eye every so often.

As the crowd thinned, Vashti caught Mr. Hintz’s eye. He smiled, excused himself from the people with whom he was speaking and made his way over to her and Sadie. Extending his hand, he gushed, “Margaret would have been so proud of you ladies. You were all like her own dear children.” He unashamedly had tear stains on his ruddy cheeks. They could see that he was exhausted, but happy for how many people had turned out for the memorial service and for how the plans had all come together.

Vashti was so touched by his grief that she felt she should try to make him feel better. “Mr. Hintz, we were honored to be included today. I imagine that Miss Blackthorne will be deeply missed by you. Didn’t you say that she was like a sister to you?”

He seemed relieved that someone was taking the lead, if only for a moment. “Yes, we grew up next door to one another.” He was dabbing his eyes as Amanda, Christina and Cybil walked up. “Miss Fetkenheuer, the band was simply wonderful. I don’t know that I have ever heard them sound better!”

“Thank you, Mr. Hintz. It was our honor to be able to perform for the memorial service.”

Pulling himself together he asked, “Is there something I can help you with, ladies?”

Vashti spoke for the group. “May we have the cornet, Mr. Hintz? We have some ideas about what to do with it.”

“You certainly may. And while we are making future plans, I have been instructed by Margaret’s attorney to invite a delegation from the band to be present at the reading of the will. This will take place at 7:00 p.m. on Monday evening here in the Founder’s Hall.”

The little ensemble was surprised but agreed that they would all be there. Then he offered to get the cornet off of the podium for them. As they approached the stage and he reached up for the case he commented, “That was a nice gesture to have a single rose in the case.” He smiled at them, but they just looked at one another.

“Mr. Hintz, I thought that you had done that,” said Vashti. Then she thought that Jack had probably brought the rose and her heart warmed at his thoughtfulness.

He took the rose out of the case, closed it, handed the case and the rose to Vashti. He looked at the ladies. “She loved roses. Thank you again, ladies. It was a wonderful service and Margaret would have been so proud of the band. I will look forward to seeing you all on Monday evening."

Vashti raised the rose to her face and breathed in its faint aroma. As they turned to go backstage they spied Jack standing in the doorway. Vashti rushed forward and blurted out, "Jack, thank you so much for getting the cornet repaired and here on time for the memorial service. And what a sweet gesture it was to bring a single rose." She beamed at her hero. Jack smiled but scratched his head.

"You are welcome, ladies. I was only too happy to be of service to you. As for the rose, I must admit that it wasn't me."

They thanked him warmly and made their way backstage to collect their instruments and belongings. Family members were gathering around. Danforth took possession of the cornet and Reggie carried his sister's French horn. They walked to the PRT and rode home with hundreds of other Philadelphians who had seen fit to come out in droves to pay their respects Margaret Blackthorne.

Back at the house Vashti changed out of her uniform and into one of her favorite and most comfortable frocks. When she came downstairs into the parlor, she found her mother reading. "You look relaxed, my darling daughter."

"I am surprisingly tired, Mother."

"An emotional day like this will take its toll. I did think that the band was magnificent, my dear."

"Thank you, Mother. We are going to try to keep the band together. It will be quite a challenge, but it means so much to all of us. I don't know what I would do if I didn't have our Tuesday rehearsals where I could play my French horn."

"You know that your father and I will do everything we can to support you in this endeavor, Vashti. We have so enjoyed hearing the band progress. It has been a joy for all of us, even Danforth and Reggie." Looking somewhat conspiratorial she continued, "I think that Danny has his eye on a couple of the ladies in the band." They laughed and passed the time until supper with pleasant banter about a myriad of subjects touching on something light, something lofty and then something amusing just like a well-programmed band concert.

Before Vashti knew it, Hettie was calling them to supper. She had cooked a hearty meal of quail roasted with bay leaf and capped with bacon. Green beans were plentiful from the garden and crusty bread was warm inside a basket. Along side of the quail were sweet pickles and spiced beets. All summer long Hettie and Mrs. Smith preserved vegetables from the ample kitchen garden. Vashti often helped, but especially loved harvesting and drying herbs. This helped the household budget and allowed for other purchases for family enjoyment.

Sunday was Hettie's day off, but there would be plenty of tasty food for the next day. Vashti and her mother took care of those things on Sundays. After their supper Father called them all together in the parlor to read Oscar Wilde's The Importance of Being Earnest. Reading plays was a common entertainment for them on Saturday evenings, often with various family members reading the roles. Vashti loved to hear her mother read these stories and thought that she could have been a great actress. Reggie would often bring them all to fits of laughter with his imitation of a British accent. They didn't finish the entire play that evening, but would save it for another evening. Then the children wished their parents a good night. Vashti kissed each of her parents' cheeks. The boys gave their mother a peck on the cheek before all ascended the staircase to the wishes of pleasant dreams.

# Chapter 22

Vashti awoke with the sun feeling refreshed. Lingering in her bed, she watched as the sun peeked his rays through her lacy curtains. The birds were beginning to sing, the air was fresh and a slight breeze brought the warm air into her room. The squirrels were chasing each other through the branches of the sycamore outside her window. "How I love Sundays," thought Vashti. "The sameness that is different every week."

She would be happy to have a relaxed Sunday. It was her family's custom to attend a church service in the morning, to linger a bit after the service to talk with friends and then return home to a light dinner. Then they might sit in the garden and read. Reggie would likely be up to some mischief or running about trying to catch butterflies. In the afternoon there would be time for tea and then they might sit on the front porch to visit with any of the neighbors who would happen to stroll by on an afternoon walk.

She got out of bed and chose her pink skirt and white shirtwaist to wear to church. As she was using the buttonhook to button up her shoes there was a light tap at the door. "Come in."

Her mother opened the door. "May I help you with your hair?"

"Thank you, Mother. That would be wonderful." They chatted as Elizabeth brushed her daughter's hair out and then caught it in a comb at the back of her head. There were a few delightful curls that bounced around refusing to be contained. They went downstairs for breakfast and then followed much of their traditional routine for the remainder of the day.

They were sitting in the parlor drinking tea when Elizabeth said, "It's much too hot in here for tea. If you will move things to the front porch I will see if there is any ice in the icebox and we shall have iced tea."

All thought this was a capital idea. Elizabeth marched to the kitchen and the others set the tea service on its tray. Prof. Smith carried the tray out to the porch while Vashti and Reggie held open the French doors. He set the tea tray down on the white wicker table. Danforth gathered some chairs around and Elizabeth appeared with a pitcher of ice. She spooned ice into each teacup to cool off what had already been poured. Then she took the teapot out of its cozy and poured the hot tea over the ice in the pitcher to chill it.

Vashti sat in the shade enjoying her tea. She held the cup in her hand and traced the lovely design with her eyes. Something was gnawing in the back of her mind but she wasn't sure what it was.

"Hello, Smith family."

There was Jack. She was so focused on her teacup that she didn't see him walking along her street. It was always such a thrill to see him!

"Hello, Jack," replied Mrs. Smith. "Would you like to join us for a little iced tea?"

"Thank you, Mrs. Smith. I would." He entered the yard through the picket fence gate and bounded up the front steps. Danforth gave up his chair and Vashti went back into the house through the French doors to fetch a cup and saucer for Jack. She was flushed with the excitement of seeing him. They hadn't really been able to talk after the memorial service. She set the cup and saucer down for her mother to pour Jack a cup of tea.

"Do you take sugar and cream in your tea, Jack?"

"I drink it plain, Mrs. Smith. I think that the tartness helps my embouchure." He was having a little fun with them, but Vashti knew that he actually thought this helped.

She watched him closely as he took a polite sip of his tea with his pinky properly extended. Suddenly she shouted, "Jack, I have another clue!"

Jack tossed his tea in the air and was trying not to wear it down the front of his suit. They all jumped and looked at Vashti.

"I'm sorry. I didn't mean to startle anyone, but I've been looking at the teacups and something has been gnawing in the back of my mind. Jack, you didn't put the single rose in the cornet case, did you? Mr. Hintz didn't put it there either. He thought that one of the band members had done it."

Jack looked at her. In fact the whole family was looking at her with her mother and her brothers raising their eyebrows in the family's questioning look.

"Don't you remember? When we picked up the cornet from the Coroners Office there was a single rose as part of the evidence. The mouthpiece was different, too. If we can find the person who purchased a single rose on both of those days we may find the murderer."

They all sat and thought this through for a few moments. Jack was the first to speak. "I think you may have something there, Vashti, but isn't this a little like hunting for a needle in a haystack?"

"Jack, you know every instrument that comes into Conn. You know it by its model number. If it has been dented you know this and you usually know how it happened too. Am I right?"

"Yes," he said slowly starting to see where she was going with this idea.

"Flower shop keepers would know their customers well enough to know who came in to buy a single rose for his lady fair. They might even teach the customer the language of flowers."

She lost Jack at this point. Prof. Smith could see that Jack was lost and stepped in.

"When I was courting Elizabeth, I would bring her different flowers to show my intentions. For example, I brought daffodils at first to show my chivalry. Then I brought amaryllis and hydrangea. White lilacs mean that my love was pure and eventually I brought red roses to declare my love. I learned the language of flowers from my father, but I also had a special flower shop where they helped me in my courtship dance." He smiled at Elizabeth.

"I think there will be a flower shop that will know who purchased those roses. Jack, we have to tell your father!"

Jack looked at Vashti over the remainder of his tea. "Do you think that someone was in love with Miss Blackthorne?"

"I don't know, but this will give them another clue worth pursuing. We have to tell your father! Now."

Richard stood up. "I'll get my hat. Vashti, you get your hat and gloves and the three of us will go to Jack's home. That is, if you would expect your father to be at home, Jack."

"I know that he is, sir, but I might ask you to wait outside so that I can give my mother a little notice of unexpected company."

"But, of course, Jack. We wouldn't want to do anything that would cause upset."

They gathered at the front door and the trio set out towards Jack's house. It was too far for Vashti to walk in her soft cotton slippers, so they took the PRT. When they got to Jack's neighborhood there were many children playing on the steps and sidewalk. There were happy voices everywhere. Vashti marveled at seeing the neighborhood where her Jack had grown up. It was boisterous. Not at all like her neighborhood and she liked it.

Two sweet girls called out, "Hi, Jack!"

He waved to them. "These are my sisters," he said, as they came running up and hugged their brother. "Erin and Rachel, I would like to you to meet Professor Smith and his daughter, Vashti."

The girls made their greeting without any shyness. Vashti took up a conversation regarding the finer points of hopscotch. Prof. Smith looked on with amusement.

"Will you wait here for just a moment while I tell my mother that we have company?"

Prof. Smith spoke up, "Of course, Jack. Tell her not to fuss. It's official police business."

Jack smiled and ran up the stairs taking two at a time. He wasn't really worried about how clean things were. His mother kept a tidy house, but with five brothers and sisters it was hard to find a quiet place sometimes. He just wanted to check out the noise level before bringing the Smiths inside.

This would also be the first time that Vashti would meet his mother. He hoped they would both like each other. Opening the door, he saw his pop wrestling with George. His sisters were playing paper dollies at the kitchen table while his mother sat near the window fanning herself.

"You're back early, son," she said.

"Well, something has come up."

Sean stopped wrestling and gave his full attention to Jack.

"I stopped to visit with Vashti and her family. She has made a discovery that may help you in the Blackthorne case." Sean was on his feet,

"I'll get my hat."

"I brought them here, Pop." Looking at his father and mother he added, "I hope that's okay. I asked them to wait downstairs so I could let you know and not surprise you."

"My heavens, this is an exciting turn of events," cried Molly, but she was smiling. "Sean, I'll take the children to the park. Jack will fetch us when you are done."

Sean was straightening his tie and smoothing his hair. "Bring them up, son. It's time your mother met the Smith family anyway."

"It's just Vashti and her father."

Sean looked at his son, pointed and said, "Go." He looked at Molly as she was smoothing her hair and gathering the children. "Well, wouldn't it be something to get a break in the case." The door opened and in walked Vashti with a pleasant smile under her sassy curls. Prof. Smith followed and Jack closed the door behind him. He made all of the introductions like an old pro and his mother beamed.

"It is lovely to meet you both, but I know that you have business to attend to and I'll be taking the children to the park to give you some peace and quiet." She mother-henned her chicks out the door and smiled as she left. So this was the precious Vashti. She liked her. Pretty, but not too pretty. Well-spoken and able to make eye contact easily. It was a good first meeting if ever so brief.

Sean invited them to be seated at the kitchen table. "May I offer you some refreshment?"

Prof. Smith spoke up, "I think that my daughter would just like to tell you what she had discovered, but thank you, Sergeant." Sean sat down across from Vashti and she told him her thoughts about the roses. He sat rubbing his chin. It could be a good lead or it could go nowhere. Right now he had nothing to go on so this would be his next move.

"Thank you for sharing this, Miss Smith. I'll follow up on it tomorrow morning. Remember to keep this information to yourselves. I'll let you know if anything comes of it."

Richard stood up and reached out to shake hands with Sean. "Come, daughter. We have delivered your message and will allow the O'Brien family to enjoy the remainder of their Sunday."

Sean and Jack saw them to the door. When they had left, Sean clapped his hand on his son's shoulder and said, "She's fine lass, Jack." Jack smiled at his father. "Go get the family from the park. Your mother will likely have some thoughts on Miss Vashti, too."

Jack bolted out the door, down the front steps and toward the park, leaping over toys and children on his way as if he heard a band playing a rousing gallop. He found his mother and siblings at the park and they walked back to the house, Jack carrying Ian on his shoulders.

Later that evening, when the youngest children had gone to sleep, Jack sat at the kitchen table with his parents. They talked about the day and Sean told Molly what had transpired with Vashti and Prof. Smith.

Turning to Jack, Molly said, "I liked her right away, Jack. I hope that we get to see more of her soon." Jack just smiled. He was glad to know that his parents liked Vashti.

"Well, I will be at Conn bright and early tomorrow. With the store having been closed on Saturday we'll probably be twice as busy, so I'll bid you a good night."

"Good night, son."

After he was out of the room, Molly looked at Sean. "What do you think of Vashti Smith?"

"I think she is a very intelligent young lady."

"Because she came up with the flower clue?"

"No. Because she is sweet on our son."

Molly gave him a playful nudge. She was glad that Sean now had something more to go on. He took his work seriously and this case was troubling to him. She could tell that it had been a worry to him. Tomorrow would be another long day for him. She made a mental note to have a bracing breakfast for him in the morning.

♫

Sean was light of step as he walked to the station. He was glad to have another lead in the case, but wondered what sort of man would murder the woman he loved. They hadn't run across any romance in Miss Blackthorne's life. Surely Stanley would have known something.

He sprang up the front steps of the station. There were no reporters there yet. That was a relief. He observed none in the lobby yet either.

"Morning, Evans."

"Morning, sir."

"Brinkman here yet?"

"In the ready room, sir. Shall I send for him?"

"Please."

Sean took off his hat and coat and hung them. He sat in his chair and squeaked over to his desk. Picking up the first of Brinkman's notebooks, he found the section devoted to Stanley and was rereading the line of questioning when Brinkman's shadow hit the door.

"Morning, Adam. Have a seat."

Brinkman entered, closed the door behind him and sat down. Sean relayed to him the visit from the Smith's and the possible clue regarding the flowers.

"Sergeant, I must say that I don't always understand the ladies."

"And you probably never will, Adam. It is our fate, I'm afraid, but then their company is mighty sweet."

It was a rare light moment in what had so far been a frustrating case.

"We'll start with flower shops near to the Founders Hall and work our way out by blocks. Get the city directory from Evans and make a list."

Adam was up and out and in and down with the book in his lap and the notebook on the edge of Sean's desk writing down addresses. In no time at all he had an even dozen.

"That will be a good start. Let's hope today we can find something to help us out."

Both men were standing. Adam opened the office door while Sean put on his coat and grabbed his hat. As they walked out he called over his shoulder, "Probably gone for the morning, Evans. I'll call in about midway through the morning."

Sean and Adam went out the front door and to a waiting police wagon. Adam gave the address to the driver since there were still no reporters to follow them. At the first store they entered, there was the lovely scent of fresh cut flowers. Beautiful gladiolas were on display in a wide variety of colors. A gentleman stepped up to the counter.

"May I help you gentlemen?"

"Are you the owner of the store, sir?"

"I am."

"Would you know if you sold a single red rose to someone twice in the last week or so?"

"That would be unusual in July. I mostly sell red roses in June. So I have not sold any in the last couple of weeks."

"Thank you for your time."

They climbed back into the wagon and proceeded to the next shop on the list. The next two shops were also unsuccessful and they were entering shop number four.

"May I help you?" came a soft voice.

Sean was looking at a very tall man with thinning hair and gold wire glasses. He would describe this man as mousy with a bushy mustache and very bushy eyebrows that bounced around like a drumstick on a tight snare drum. "Yes, sir. Are you the owner of this store?"

"I am." He patted the flower he'd been tending and tugged his tie.

"Have you sold a single rose to someone in the last week?"

"Ah, a lovely rosoideae of the genus *Rosa*. Do you know what species of rose it was?

The policemen looked at each other and shrugged.

"There is a lady who comes in here every Friday and purchases one red rose for as long as I have them. I can't get them year around, but I have a farmer who is able to grow them longer than most local suppliers."

"Do you know her name?"

"I don't."

"Can you describe her?"

"I think she is probably in her forties. Rather non-descript really. Not the sort of face you would pick out of a crowd." He eyebrows bounced.

"She comes on Fridays, you say. What time?"

"Always after four o'clock. Is there a problem, sirs?" More tie tugging ensued.

"We are just gathering information. Thank you, Mr. . . . . um."

"Yingling. Leonard Yingling."

"Mr. Yingling, might you be able to accompany us to police headquarters? We know so little about roses, perhaps you could identify it."

"Oh, my! I'd have to leave the store in Mrs. Yingling's care." His eyebrows bounced around like the timpani part to Haydn's drum roll symphony. He fiddled with his tie while the moustache twitched. "Perhaps I could ask her to do that. It's rather unusual. My customers are so used to seeing me, not her, with my flowers."

"Please, Mr. Yingling. It would help us a great deal."

"Yes. Well, let me, um, let me speak with my wife. Just a minute, please." He scurried off to the back of the shop.

"I wasn't thinking that this person was a woman, Brinkman. That hardly makes any sense."

"If you don't mind me saying so, not much about this case does, Sergeant."

The little mousy man returned followed by his wife. Sean was amazed to see a mousy woman with bushy eyebrows following Mr. Yingling.

"Mrs. Yingling will watch the shop, gentlemen. Could we hurry? I do need to be back for my customers." He had his hat in his hands and was fingering the brim in a rhythm that matched his eyebrows.

"We will get you back to your store as soon as possible, Mr. Yingling. Thank you for helping us."

The three men marched out to the police wagon and headed across town to police head quarters. Sean led the way to the office of Dr. Mortimer Harrison, Coroner. Brinkman strode ahead to open the door. O'Brien entered followed by Yingling and Brinkman.

"Doc?" he called out, as there was no one in the front office. Doc Harrison's head appeared from behind the door. "Sergeant! I wasn't expecting anyone. I'm sorry."

"That's okay, Doc. I didn't call ahead. This is Mr. Yingling. He owns a flower store and I would like him to look at that rose from the Blackthorne case."

"It's right back here, you can all come with me. This evidence has been processed."

The little parade entered a room in the back of the office. There sat the rose right next to space where the cornet case had been. The rose was in sad shape as Mr. Yingling gently took it in his hands. "A very lovely example of a *Pimpinellifoliae*."

Sean watched his eyebrows timpani away at each word. He almost hugged the fragile rose. "Is it one of yours, Mr. Yingling?"

"Yes, yes, it is," he said, wistfully. "Do you see this angular cut on the bottom of the stem? I cut all of my roses in this manner. They drink in more water and last much longer. However, this specimen is very delicate and it is quite late in the growing season for a William III." Eyebrows flourishing.

"I thought that was a Pimpin - something - or other?"

"Sergeant, *Pimpinellifoliae* is the botanical grouping. This is an old Scotch variety of rose called a William III."

O'Brien just nodded. "But you did sell this rose, William III, to the mystery lady. Is that accurate?"

"Yes, Sergeant. That is my cut at the base. I don't think anyone else in town is as careful with their rosebuds as I." Eyebrows puckered and mustache twitching.

"Thank you, Mr. Yingling. That helps us a great deal." Turning to Dr. Harrison. "Thanks, Doc. That's all we need."

O'Brien led the way out and back to the police wagon, with Brinkman bringing up the rear. They dropped Yingling off at his shop, thanking him for helping in the investigation.

Once he was out of earshot, Brinkman looked at O'Brien, "He's an interesting character. I wrote down William III. There is no way I could spell that fancy flower word to describe a rose!"

"That's fine, Adam. At least we know where the rose was purchased now." The longer you do this job, the more interesting people you meet. At least he doesn't seem to be dangerous."

The two men went back to the district, but by the end of the day, there was no more new information. At least they could always watch Yingling's flower shop on Friday.

# Chapter 23

Vashti was rushing through her supper.

"Vashti, slow down! It's very improper for a lady to take such large bites."

"uhfwefiosdzovhjh"

"And don't talk with your mouth full. What has gotten into you?"

Daubing her lips with her napkin, Vashti managed an intelligible sentence. "I'm sorry Mother. I'm just so excited about the reading of Miss Blackthorne's Last Will and Testament. I've never been to anything like this before. I can't imagine what is in it and why the band members have been invited."

"Settle down, Vashti. No daughter of mine is going to have digestive trouble in public. Take smaller bites and chew everything carefully. You have plenty of time."

Danforth was her escort this evening. He would probably get a game of billiards in while he waited. Soon enough brother and sister were walking to the PRT stop.

"Who do you think will be at this reading, Sis?"

"I would expect someone from the Blackthorne Bunting Works. Maybe someone from her church will be there, and then the band members. As far as I know she had no family. Her parents died in a boating accident when she was about my age."

"You'll have some interesting stories to tell tonight."

They rode the PRT happy in each other's company. Danforth knew that Vashti was showing some interest in Jack O'Brien, so he didn't know how much longer he would enjoy her company like this.

At the downtown stop for the Founders Hall, they disembarked and took the short walk to the stage entrance. Entering, they stood for a moment to let their eyes adjust.

Mr. Hintz was there with his wife. Christina, Amanda, Sadie and Cybil were already there. Bishop Beecher was there with his wife, too. Mr. Hintz spoke up, "I think everyone is here. There are seats inside the hall for everyone and Margaret's attorney, Mr. Ryan, is waiting for us."

"I was just going to drop my sister off and come back for her later," Danforth and Alexander Fetkenheuer nodded. He had accompanied the other band members to the reading.

"I think this will take a little more than an hour if you would like to meet right back here," Mr. Hintz suggested. Danforth and Alexander nodded and took their leave.

"Ladies, won't you please come into the hall?" Mr. Hintz directed them toward the door that led to the main floor. Once inside they found the others already seated. He showed them to their seats.

In front of the block of chairs was a heavy mahogany table. On the table was a faun colored, legal sized leather portfolio. Mr. Hintz escorted his wife to a seat in the middle of the front row and then strode over to the table.

"Ladies and gentlemen, thank you for being here this evening. Our purpose is to hear the reading of Margaret Blackthorne's Last Will and Testament. I would like to introduce her attorney, Mr. Thomas Ryan."

They all sat quietly, certain that this was not the time to applaud. Mr. Ryan had been seated in the front row, but now stood and made his way to the table where he was seated. He drew the portfolio to himself, opened it and began to read.

"I, Margaret Mary Blackthorne, of the city and county of Philadelphia, in the state of Pennsylvania, do hereby make, publish and declare this my Last Will and Testament in the name and form following, that I do say:

ARTICLE I. I commit my soul. . . ."

Vashti was amazed at the formality of this event. It was very serious indeed. She would have much to share when she returned home this evening and many questions, too.

"ARTICLE II. It is my desire to be buried in the same cemetery as my parents. I wish that in all arrangements for my funeral . . ."

Vashti's mind was in a whirl. She had no idea of what to expect and her brain was suddenly filled with questions. What must the other band members seated next to her be thinking? She couldn't ask them. Proper etiquette precluded her from even making a glance in their direction.

"ARTICLE III. I direct that all my debts, funeral and testamentary charges be paid as soon after my decease as conveniently as can be done . . ."

Wow! thought Vashti. It seems like everything in a persons life was going to be covered.

" . . . are satisfied that it would be my wish to have paid." Mr. Ryan stopped for a moment, poured himself a glass of water and took a sip. Then he continued.

"ARTICLE IV. Section 1. I give and bequeath unto my sister Alice Marie Blackthorne, if she survives me, the sum of fifty thousand dollars.

Section 2. If my said sister, Alice Marie Blackthorne, shall die before me I direct my executors and trustees to direct this share to the Margaret Blackthorne Foundation, Inc.
Section 3. I give and bequeath my home to Robert Hintz for his use. This lot together with all furniture, clothing, silver, works of art, bric-a-brac household goods and equipment are given to him to do

with as he sees proper. I direct Mr. Hintz to keep on my driver, Stanley Robertson, and to care for him in his old age.

ARTICLE V. I give to 'The Trustees of Estate and Property of Christ Church a hundred thousand dollars to be used . . .'

At this Vashti's head began to spin. She couldn't even conceive these large sums of money. How she yearned to look at her friends to see their expressions. They had to be thinking the same thing. Could it be that Miss Blackthorne had given money to the band so that it could continue? She was trying to stay focused, but she thought that everyone in the room was probably experiencing the same excitement and general disbelief.

Mr. Ryan stopped once again to take a drink of water.

"ARTICLE VI. Section 1. I give and bequeath Blackthorne Bunting Works to Robert Hintz. He has always been like a brother to me and I know he will run the company in a fair, equitable and profitable fashion.
Section 2. I give and bequeath one year's wages to all of my Blackthorne Bunting Works employees.

ARTICLE VII. Section 1. I give and bequeath one hundred thousand dollars to the Margaret Blackthorne Foundation, Inc.

Section 2. I give and bequeath all of the remainder of my investments to the Margaret Blackthorne Foundation, Inc. to be managed by the trustees. The interest from these investments is to be used in the best interest of immigrant women in the city of Philadelphia.

Section 3. I further give and bequeath to the Margaret Blackthorne Foundation, Inc. the sum of fifty thousand dollars to be invested by the trustees and the interest used for the perpetuation of the Betsy Ross All-Lady Silver Cornet Band. This will include the continued use of Founders Hall for rehearsals and concerts, maintenance of the music library, uniform, instruments and whatever else they deem necessary to continue the legacy of bettering woman through band music."

Vashti could not believe her ears and would have thought that she was dreaming except that Sadie had grabbed her arm with such force that she was starting to lose the feeling in her right hand. She patted Sadie's hand a couple of times and the grip mercifully loosened. She could see Sadie's head bobbling out of the corner of her eye.

"IN WITNESS WHEREOF, I have here set unto my hand this twelfth day of January, Eighteen hundred and ninety-eight.
*Margaret Mary Blackthorne*

Mr. Ryan straightened the papers and closed them in the portfolio once again. Looking up, he could see how stunned those gathered were. "This concludes the reading of Margaret Blackthorne's Last Will and Testament. No doubt you have a number of questions. Mr. Hintz and I will meet with each of the groups and individuals named herein. We will work out the future details. May I suggest that you just continue on in your normal routines for the time being?"

Mr. Hintz stood again. "I would like to thank you all for coming here this evening. As Mr. Ryan has stated, he and I will be in touch with each group represented here this evening in the near future."

A beehive-like buzz began in the hall as people began to talk to one another. Vashti looked at her band friends. "She made it possible for us to continue with the band! Here we were worrying about how this was going to come about and she had already taken care of us!" Amanda, Christina and Cybil smiled while Sadie bobbled her head. They were all amazed. What a generous lady Miss Blackthorne was continuing to be! They chattered away as they walked to the backstage area to await their escorts.

Mr. Hintz and his wife found the ensemble backstage. "Now you know why you were invited, ladies. I knew about all of these provisions when Margaret signed her will last year. Mrs. Hintz and I are so pleased that the band will continue."

Vashti was thrilled, but she was puzzled, too. "Mr. Hintz, I didn't know that Miss Blackthorne had a sister."

"Yes, her sister Alice. Alas, we don't know where she is. Mr. Ryan is working on finding her. I grew up next door to Alice as well, but she didn't want anything to do with the company and left before Margaret started the band."

At that moment Danforth and Alexander came through the stage door. The air inside was electric with excitement. Danforth gathered his sister and Alexander gathered the others to escort them home. They said their goodbyes until band rehearsal tomorrow evening.

On the PRT Vashti chattered away, talking about the evening. Danforth was enjoying listening to her and was equally thrilled to know that the band would be able to continue. Miss Blackthorne had been remarkably generous to everyone around her. "Someday I hope I will be able to be as philanthropic as Miss Blackthorne. The problem is, I don't know yet what kind of work I want to do," he offered.

"Couldn't you be a billiard master? I think you do very well in your games."

"Oh, Vashti, I'm a very good billiard player, but that's no way to earn one's way. Mother really doesn't like me playing games of chance. I think I may follow Father's example and go to college to teach something. I'll need to be making some decisions on that soon." He sat quietly for a few minutes before probing his sister's mind. "And what about you, sister of mine? You seem to be enjoying the company of Jack O'Brien a great deal. Do you hear wedding bells in your future?"

Vashti laughed. She knew that most of her friends were hoping to catch the eye and heart of some eligible young man. She was tremendously fond of Jack, but she had a secret dream that she now chose to share with her brother.

"Can you keep a secret?"

Danforth used the family eyebrow motion to show interest. "Of course."

"What I really want to do is audition for Helen May Butler to play in her band. She's known as 'The Female Sousa' and her band is top notch."

"Why, that's a splendid idea! I remember hearing her band! Have you told this to anyone else?"

"Not a soul. You'll keep my secret, won't you?"

"I'll do better than that, Vashti. I'll help you in any way I can so you can achieve your dream!"

Vashti hugged her brother's arm. The PRT stopped and they got off to walk in the warm evening air, watching the moths dance around the street lamps.

As they approached the house, they could see Reggie outside with his jars trying to catch fireflies. If he could get a few in a jar, they would glow, but he would release them after a while so they didn't die. He called a greeting as brother and sister came up the walk and entered the house. They could see him heading for the back door to learn how their evening had been. All the Smith children were curious, but Reggie was the only one interested in bugs.

They entered the Smith home to greetings from their parents and Reggie. They were all waiting expectantly to hear about the evening. Danforth listened as his sister related the events of the last few hours and he rejoiced in the unique person she had become. He liked the way that she thought and the interesting conversation that she brought to gatherings.

They all converged in the front parlor where Mrs. Smith was doing needlework and Prof. Smith was reading poetry aloud. He stopped when they entered. Her parents could see the excitement on Vashti's pretty face.

"Father, have you been to a reading of a Last Will and Testament? Maybe for your parents?"

"I have not, though I certainly heard about a few of them. My parents never had much money, so there was no need to have a will and, even if they would have had a will, it would not have been nearly as interesting as this one!"

"It was so interesting to hear about how Miss Blackthorne provided for all the groups with which she was associated." Vashti stopped for a moment, thinking.

Her mother knew that something was tickling her brain. "What is it, Vashti?"

After a Grand Pause moment, Vashti looked at her parents and said, "Miss Blackthorne has a sister. Did you know that?"

They all looked at one another. Her mother broke the silence. "That's certainly news to me," eyebrows high with surprise. "Was she there tonight?"

"No. Mr. Hintz said that they didn't know where she was. Mr. Ryan was looking for her. Doesn't that strike you as odd?"

"Not all families are very close, Vashti. Your father and I have made a conscious choice to have a welcoming home. All three of you children have been here to meet the interesting people we enjoy having as guests. Your friends are part of those gatherings too. We hope that stimulating conversation is very much appreciated by you. It is a wonderful way to pass the evening and our family appreciates thoughts and ideas."

Her father smiled at his wife. "And we have certainly had plenty of exciting conversation today. It's enough for the day. Let's retire and all get some well-deserved rest."

All nodded in agreement and went off to their bedrooms with many fascinating thoughts dancing in their heads.

# Chapter 24

Elisabeth was thrilled to see it raining. The rain would help her garden since her hollyhocks were starting to look a little peaked. It was a lazy day around the Smith house. Vashti was anxious to get to band rehearsal that evening. She pondered the possibility of an instrument breaking and being able to make a trip to the Conn store to see Jack.

At dinner the conversation covered many topics. Her father was waxing poetic about the Shakespeare play he was currently reading. He would be teaching a class on Shakespeare in the fall and was studying several of the bard's historical plays. Vashti knew The Tempest, but was unaware of most of the other literature. Her father was talking about Henry VI, Part 1. She wasn't very focused, but listened sideways to the relationship of the real King Henry.

A pleasant afternoon ensued as the rain stopped, the sun dried things out and the hollyhocks were happily holding droplets of water on their petals. Reggie was running around looking for toads. Elizabeth liked to encourage the children in their interests, but she found Reginald's to be a bit of a challenge. She had banned most of them from the house, but a few were allowed inside if contained. Reggie had appropriated a number of Mason jars just for this purpose.

"I think I will practice a bit for the rehearsal tonight. Amanda will probably go over some of our past pieces in the folder, but I hope we'll get a new piece to learn as well." She went upstairs to her room and began by playing a carefully crafted warm-up and then ran through all of her major and minor scales.

Miss Blackthorne had repeatedly told them that, "A fine band could play all of its scales." Miss Blackthorne's voice came into her head. Vashti stopped playing and knew it would take a while to get over this sadness.

She took out one of her older lesson books and began to play the pieces that she most enjoyed, just for the sheer joy of playing. She loved the way the French horn felt in her hands. It was cool and soft all at the same time. Vashti didn't want to tax her lip too much before rehearsal so she wiped down the French horn and returned it safely to its case.

♫

Before she knew it, Danforth was at her side and she was off to band rehearsal. Stepping inside the stage door, Vashti was strangely comforted by the cacophony of warm-ups that greeted her. It was a reassuring sign that the band would continue.

Rehearsal went well. Amanda did a tremendous job and was applauded at the end by her musicians. She thanked them for their support and asked for their continued support as she learned her new role as their conductor.

Vashti found Amanda after the rehearsal. "Amanda! You did such a lovely job with rehearsal tonight!" Sadie was just joining them and bobbled her approval.

"There's so much to learn! I just scheduled the pieces that Miss Blackthorne taught us. All of that musicianship is what we learned from her. I'm just starting the band and staying out of the way." The friends could tell that she was overwhelmed with emotion, but was resolved to learn to lead. This was one of the things that she liked about her band friends. They were all there giving their support to Amanda, but they would also face their challenges the same way, straight on, in an effort to discover what it took to be successful.

They were standing around Amanda giving her encouragement when Vashti saw Sadie, who was the tallest, looking off toward the stage door. Following her glance she spied Mr. Hintz approaching the ensemble.

“Good evening, ladies. I heard the very end of your rehearsal and the band is sounding wonderful. Miss Fetkenheuer, you are to be commended.”

“Thank you, Mr. Hintz. I am surrounded by very fine musicians.”

“Indeed, you are. Was everything in place for your rehearsal this evening?”

“Yes, it was. Thank you.”

“Ladies, I would like to meet with the five of you and Mr. Ryan to explain how the Margaret Blackthorne Trust is set up. When might we be able to do that?”

Looking around at each other they waited to see who would offer a suggestion. Vashti was the first. “May I invite you to tea at my house tomorrow?”

“That would be lovely, Vashti,” said Amanda. “You’re sure it won’t be an intrusion? My house is filled with father’s piano students coming and going throughout the day.”

“I am certain it will be just fine. May I suggest an early tea at 3:00 p.m.?”

Sadie bobbled and the others nodded their enthusiastic agreement. The rehearsal soon broke up and all went their own directions. When Vashti and Danforth returned to the Smith abode, they joined the rest of the family in the front parlor where Reggie was trying to beat his father at chess.

Vashti recounted her evening’s rehearsal and the invitation for an afternoon tea on the morrow, looking to her mother for approval. “That’s a lovely idea, my dear. You and I shall go in the morning to find some tasty *petits fours*. Gentlemen of the house, I shall make certain there are enough for each of you, as well. How would you like to serve this, Vashti?”

"Well, I think if we had tea on the porch overlooking your garden, we could have the band members outside and another table just inside for the family members. We should plan for whomever escorts my friends as well. That arrangement wouldn't be a breech of etiquette, would it? There isn't anything secret about this meeting. It's just a pleasant way for Mr. Hintz and Mr. Ryan to teach us how the Trust is going to take care of things for the band."

"I think the gentlemen should gather in your father's study and allow Mr. Ryan and Mr. Hintz to talk to the band members first. Then I'll see to it that everyone gathers for tea. Will that suit you, Vashti?"

"Thank you, Mother! That will be wonderful!"

# Chapter 25

The next day dawned bright and beautiful like the trio strain of a D.W. Reeves march. Hettie was informed of the afternoon tea and that Vashti and Mrs. Smith would do the shopping for the *petits fours*. All she needed to prepare would be the tea service for fifteen to twenty guests. Hettie loved it when the Smiths had company. She whistled her favorite songs while bustling about the kitchen. The happy strains of "When Irish Eyes Are Smilin'," "When Clancy Lowers the Boom," "Danny Boy," all floated out of the kitchen.

Vashti and her mother donned their hats and gloves and headed out to the bakery for *petits fours.* They chatted about the tea and Mrs. Smith reviewed the etiquette of serving tea. She was pleased that her daughter had offered to host this tea, not just because of learning about how the band would continue, but for the valuable experience of being a good hostess.

When the ladies returned to the house with the delicate bakery items, they saw that Hettie had the tea service laid out beautifully. Hettie took the tasty morsels from Vashti. "My, these are beautiful!"

"There will be more than enough for you to have some too, Hettie."

"Thank you, Mrs. Smith! You do spoil me." Hettie smiled at her employer. One of the great things about working for the Smiths was that they treated her like family. She knew from others in her neighborhood that this was very unusual.

With the preparations made, they all awaited their afternoon company with excitement.

♫

Sadie, Christina, Cybil and Amanda all arrived at the same time escorted by Alexander, Amanda's brother, who ran off into the garden to chase bugs with Reggie. In short order Mr. Hintz arrived with Mr. Ryan. Vashti invited her guests to be seated in the parlor to hear the gentlemen speak and that tea would be served afterword.

Mr. Ryan talked about the Trustees and how they were to do everything possible to keep the Betsy Ross All-Lady Silver Cornet Band going strong. "It will be of great benefit to have elections every other year to create a band board. The board would approve Miss Fetkenheuer as the new conductor. Then you should stagger the elections so that a board member would serve three years, but every two years there would be an election. In this way you will be able to involve new members and still have some of the ladies who would have been on the board for a little longer time to lead the way."

These suggestions were all accepted and the process of communication between the band board and the Trust was established. In short order Vashti became the hostess and suggested moving on to the porch for tea. Hetti was pushing a cart with the tea service toward the tables. Professor Smith was helping to carry out the *petits fours*. Elisabeth had corralled the younger boys and was now at Mr. Hintz's side.

"Do you mind if I invite Stanley in for tea? We would certainly welcome him."

"You could certainly ask him, Mrs. Smith, but I have tried to include Stanley in family events in the past week. He says that he is employed by me and that he is working."

"Well, I think I'll ask Danforth to take a *petits four* out to him."

"That would be very kind of you, Mrs. Smith. I think he would be delighted to accept it."

As Vashti was pouring the tea for everyone, she saw Danforth carry a cup of tea and a couple of tempting cakes out to Stanley, who was caught off guard and accepted them with a smile. He looked toward the porch and smiled a "thank you" at Vashti.

Inside the French doors Mr. Hintz was making small talk with Prof. Smith about Shakespeare. Vashti caught a bit of their conversation and was watching to see that all her guests had ample refreshments. She was tracing the lovely roses on the teacups when she suddenly stood bolt upright, overturning her teacup and causing everyone to stop and stare.

"I know who did it! I know who the murderer is! Mr. Hintz, can you take me in your carriage?"

"Certainly, but where?"

"To the police station first. Come on, ladies, let's go."

The band members rushed into the hallway with Vashti urging them to move in double tempo. Danforth grabbed his hat and they all rushed down the front steps, out the gate and to the carriage. Stanley was surprised but managed to hold open the carriage door. Mr. Hintz and the five band members climbed inside and Danforth and Mr. Ryan climbed up top with Stanley who had deposited his teacup and plate in Prof. Smith's hands at the curb.

The bays leaped to a trot at a snap of the reins. Stanley knew right where to go and drove through the streets with skill and great care. He knew something was afoot and Danforth told him that his sister had discovered who Miss Blackthorne's murderer was so they were going to the police station to tell Sgt. O'Brien.

At the police station Stanley stopped the carriage and Danforth jumped down to open the door. Mr. Hintz and Vashti exploded out of the carriage and bounded up the steps into the lobby.

"Is Sergeant O'Brien here?"

Hearing the bustle he pushed back from his desk in his squeeky chair and walked into the lobby area. "Hello, Miss Smith, Mr. Hintz. How may I help you?"

"Sergeant O'Brien, I know who the murderer is. You have to come with us."

He looked at this slip of a girl who was all out of breath. Her hair was a little wild since she had forgotten her hat and she didn't have on her gloves, either. Had she been by herself he might not have taken her too seriously, but Mr. Hintz was with her so something must certainly be up.

"Evans, find Brinkman! Miss Smith, Mr. Hintz, please come into my office."

The reporters were suddenly electrified. If he didn't act quickly they'd be asking all manner of questions and making a mess of things. He ushered them in and closed the door. "Who is it, Vashti?" There was a knock at the door and Brinkman entered.

"We have to go to the Conn store before she leaves."

"Who is it we're after?"

"I'll explain along the way."

Brinkman opened the door and they marched out through the swinging doors and the lobby area past the reporters and down the front steps. Brinkman helped Vashti into the police wagon, climbed up himself, followed by O'Brien. Mr. Hintz ran back to the carriage, telling Stanley to follow.

It was a short drive, but the police wagon and the handsome blue carriage with the matched bays racing through the streets caught the attention of many along the way. Stanley was holding on to the bay horses, who were thrilled at the chance to run. The band members were jostled about inside. Vashti was bouncing around wildly in the police wagon, her hair more unruly than ever.

At the Conn store O'Brien jumped down to the sidewalk and assessed the situation. Brinkman handed Vashti down and then joined them. Mr. Hintz was out of the carriage as were the rest of the group.

O'Brien took charge of the situation. "I'll go in first with Miss Smith, Patrolman Brinkman, Mr. Hintz. I'll send for you when I'm ready. Stay out here until then. Understand?"

His tone was clipped, but they all nodded except for Sadie, of course.

The four seekers revolved through the shiny brass door, popping out on the sales floor: O'Brien first, Vashti second, Mr. Hintz third and Brinkman bringing up the rear. Mr. Ritberger was in his office but noticed them right away. Catching O'Brien's eye, he signaled that he would be down right away.

O'Brien and the others kept walking and met him in the passageway. "May we speak in your office?"

"Certainly," he said executing a crisp about-face to allow the others to enter first. He followed and once inside, closed the door.

"Mr. Ritberger, is Mrs. Tudor here today?"

"Yes, she is." His face was distressed.

"Would you ask her to come to your office, please?"

Ritberger left the office in a whirl and ran to the back of the shop where he found her. He tried to keep his voice calm.

"Mrs. Tudor, would you come with me to my office, please?"

She didn't look up but mumbled a "yes" in his direction and followed. He opened the door for her and she walked up the three steps and into the face of Henry Hintz.

"Alice, is that you?"

She startled and, looking at him, pulled back a bit and bumped into Mr. Ritberger, causing her to move toward the center of the room.

"I'm Henry Hintz. We grew up next door to each other. Do you remember me?"

Mrs. Tudor was fiddling with her work smock and staring at the plush office rug. She was chewing her lower lip, but not making any eye contact.

Mr. Ritberger spoke up first, "Can I ask what this is all about?"

O'Brien spoke. "Mrs. Tudor, do you know anything about Margaret Blackthorne's death? We have reason to believe that you are her sister, and we have further reason to suspect that you were involved in her murder. Have you anything to say in your defense?"

Mrs. Tudor raised her eyes slowly, looking back and forth from O'Brien to Hintz. Then she stared at the ground and began to sob silently.

"Brinkman, get Mr. Ryan in here."

Brinkman bolted out of the office, running into Jack as he swung the door open and pinning him against the wall. "Sorry, Jack!" he said, pushing him out of the way.

Jack looked into the office to see Vashti staring back at him. He was about to enter when he spied his father and sensed that something was up. He closed the door and went back to the store where he was nearly run down by Brinkman *and* Ryan this time. The band members were in the store now and they all gathered around Jack. "Vashti says she knows who the murderer is Jack!"

"Is that what's going on in there?"

"We think so."

Ryan entered the office where he found Mrs. Tudor seated on one of the green leather chairs. He walked over to the distraught woman and said, "I'm Thomas Ryan, Margaret Blackthorne's attorney. Are you her sister?"

Mrs. Tudor looked at him and sobbed, “I never wanted to own a business. I just wanted to live the life of a happily married lady.”

Mr. Hintz spoke up. “It is you, Alice. I remember hearing you say that many times when Margaret first founded Blackthorne Bunting Works.”

O’Brien took over. “Mrs. Tudor, I’m afraid I’ll have to take you down to the station for questioning. Mr. Ryan, you will come with me. Miss Smith, Mr. Hintz, Mr. Ritberger and Brinkman, I would like to speak with you outside.”

They trooped into the squeezy hallway.

“Brinkman, I will get an address for her home or rooming house and then I want you to go over there and search for clues. Take Mr. Hintz and Miss Smith with you. Use a call box to let me know if you find anything.”

Brinkman nodded.

“Mr. Hintz, may we use your carriage for official police business?”

“Absolutely!”

“Mr. Ritberger, I’m going to have to leave the ladies band members here for the time being. Can you accommodate them somehow?”

“I certainly can, and I have an address for Mrs. Tudor if she won’t give it to you.”

“Good. Let’s get going.”

O’Brien didn’t think it necessary to humiliate Mrs. Tudor by putting handcuffs on her. He just led her out to the waiting police wagon and helped her up. They were in the heart of downtown Philadelphia and a crowd had gathered.

Brinkman took charge of Vashti and Mr. Hintz, and headed over to Mrs. Tudor’s boarding house.

Vashti's cheeks were flushed from the excitement. Stanley drove to the boarding house with a sense of urgency, but with soft hands on the reins. Brinkman sat across from Vashti and Hintz. He was amazed at this young lady and hoped they would find something in Mrs. Tudor's room to help solve this crime. This was his first murder investigation and he was certain he would never forget it. Roses, cornets and band beauties. This one was a doozy.

At the boarding house the three riders spilled out of the carriage in an orderly sort of way.
Brinkman, as the official investigator, led the way, but he needed to step lively to keep ahead of Vashti. She clearly had the bit between her teeth. He liked her spirit.

He pounded the matte black doorknocker and waited pensively like a V7 chord in a Herman Bellstedt cadenza. The door opened to reveal a sturdy woman who, he estimated, was comfortably in her sixties.

"May I help you?" She was clearly surprised to see a patrolman on her doorstep.

"Yes ma'am. I'm Patrolman Brinkman, here on official police business. This is Henry Hintz from the Blackthorne Bunting Works and Miss Smith from the Betsy Ross All-Lady Silver Cornet Band. May we come in?"

"But, of course," she said, gliding the door open in an inviting fashion. "I'm Mrs. Landsmeyer, the proprietress of this establishment."

Brinkman took off his hat and turned toward Mrs. Landsmeyer as she closed the door behind them. "Mrs. Landsmeyer, you have a boarder by the name of Alice Tudor. Is that correct?" He had extracted a notebook from his pocket, perched it on top of his cap and was ready to write.

"Yes, Mrs. Tudor boards here."

“Have you noticed any unusual behavior from her lately?”

“She is a very unusual personality. She takes all of her meals in her room and seldom speaks to any of the other boarders. She’s a widow, poor dear. I don’t think she ever got over the loss of her husband.”

“Did she tell you this?”

“Well, no. I received a telegram from Mr. C.G. Conn asking me to take in this bereaved widow. My late husband, Oscar Landsmeyer, was a band musician. He had quite a good lip for the trombone. I knew the Conn Company, so I was certainly going to take her in.”

Hintz quizzed, “Did she pay her rent or did it come from another source?”

“I don’t know who paid it, but a messenger came every month with payment. You know I had to charge extra for meals in her room, but it was never a problem. Is she alright? I would hate to lose a good boarder like her.” At that point she turned a skeleton key in the lock and pushed open the door. The trio of visitors peered into the room. Brinkman entered. “Don’t touch anything,” he instructed.

The room was dark from the draperies being closed. He pulled back one of drapes and hooked it behind the decorative metal loop designed for this purpose. The room was tidy, but stuffy.

“Did you clean the room, Mrs. Landsmeyer?”

“Goodness, no! I would bring a tray to the door with her meals. She took the tray from me and it would appear back in the kitchen during the night. I never entered the room.”

Suddenly Vashti’s hand gripped Brinkman’s arm with a purpose. While he was contemplating the grip that was cutting the blood off to his hand, he followed Vashti’s other hand. The second hand was pointing to a cornet mouthpiece.

The trio stepped over to the roll top desk where the mouthpiece was sitting on its rim. Vashti broke the silence. “It’s a C.G. Conn Benjamin Bent model. This is the mouthpiece that was supposed to be in the case with the presentation cornet.”

Brinkman wrote this all down and then very carefully raised the cover of the desk. Inside were various and sundry bottles and vials. All were clearly labeled. Brinkman thought this looked a lot like the shelves at the druggists he had visited.

“Is this your desk, Mrs. Landsmeyer?”

“No, sir. She brought that with her.”

Hintz weighed in. “I remember now. Alice was married to a man who was a doctor. This looked like it may have been his desk.”

“And there’s a bottle of arsenic,” whispered Vashti.

“That would explain how she was able to use arsenic and we couldn’t trace it. This must have belonged to her husband.” Slapping his notebook closed and stuffing it in his coat pocket, he carefully closed the roll top.

“Let’s go back to the station. Mrs. Landsmeyer, I want you to close and lock this door behind us. Do not tell anyone about this visit. There will be a number of policemen here in short order. Your boarders will likely have questions and you can tell them about this visit after the officers have left. Thank you, ma’am.”

Out they went and back to the station, the bays prancing proudly as if they knew the crime was solved.

♫

Later that evening, Mr. Hintz invited everyone to the Blackthorne Bunting Works where he had the Pick-Penn Company Band playing while serving up celebratory ice cream and sarsparilla. When the band finished playing George Southwell's *Victory Overture,* Sgt. O'Brien 'ahemed' a few times to get everyone's attention.

"I just want to thank Mr. Hintz for having everyone here this evening. While we certainly mourn the loss of Margaret Blackthorne, it is important for our city to know that the murderer has been apprehended."

"You will probably like to know that Alice Tudor gave us a full confession. We do, however, think that she is not of sound mind. It seems that she had suffered so many losses that it made her unstable. She is currently under medical care. It is likely that she will not go to jail but will be in an institution for the criminally insane. Fortunately, Margaret Blackthorne's Last Will and Testament will provide for her care. Now on a much lighter note, I give you Mr. Hintz."

Hintz smiled at the applause and held his hand up to quiet the crowd. "I am glad to be through this murder investigation. The sorrow I have at losing my dear friend Margaret cannot possibly be expressed. Nonetheless, I know that she rests in peace thanks to the hard work of Sgt. O'Brien, Patrolman Brinkman, the Philadelphia Police Department and Miss Vashti Smith."

The happy gathering applauded again. Vashti was seated next to her Jack enjoying an ice cream. Her band friends were there as well. Sadie was bob, bob, bobbling along and when the applause died down she spoke up like a fanfare trumpet. "Vashti, how did you know Mrs. Tudor was the murderess?"

Vashti was suddenly in the limelight. She set down her ice cream, smoothed the front of her frock and addressed the crowd. "There was a rose found at the scene of the murder. When I was having tea with my family I was tracing the rose pattern on the teacup with my eyes. I realized that no one was looking into the rose and the cornet was getting all of the attention. Sgt. O'Brien and Patrolman Brinkman visited a lot of florists to see if they could find out who was buying those flowers."

"We brought the florist down to the station house and he identified her," interjected O'Brien.

Vashti continued. "At the memorial service I recalled Mr. Hintz saying that Miss Blackthorne's favorite flower was the rose, but none of us sent that single rose."

Hintz piped in, "We didn't know how the funds from one of Margaret's accounts was administered. Through some very keen detective work Sgt. O'Brien and Patrolman Brinkman found out that a messenger from the Pick-Penn Bank brought the funds to the boarding house. That messenger was Seamus O'Flarrity here."

Mr. Ritberger entered the conversation. "The reason that I didn't know that Mrs. Tudor and Miss Blackthorne were sisters is that I was asked by Mr. C.G. Conn through a telegram to offer Mrs. Tudor a job. Miss Blackthorne must have asked him to do that for her."

Mrs. Landsmeyer offered, "I got a similar telegram from Mr. Conn."

Hintz spoke up again. "We didn't know it was through the Pick-Penn Bank, because that is normally for employees. Margaret's father had been an employee of Pick-Penn. The bank was so good to her when her parents had died that she never moved her bank accounts, preferring to give them her business. Alice was never very excited about her sister being in business and then starting an all-ladies band. I think Margaret kept a close eye on her sister over the years. Margaret did these loving things to help her sister out but without her sister having to admit to knowing an 'uppity woman'."

"So no one knew that Miss Blackthorne was actually helping her sister. This afternoon as I served tea I was listening to father extol the virtues of Shakespeare's Henry the VI, Part I. I was enjoying the conversation, thinking of Henry and, once again, tracing that rose pattern on the teacups when I realized that Henry was a Tudor and that the crest for the Tudors was a rose. Roses, . . . Alice Tudor. It had to be her."

Brinkman spoke up. "When we found the Benjamin Bent cornet mouthpiece, we knew we had solved the case."

Sadie bobbled, "How did you know it was the right cornet mouthpiece?"

"Jack and I went down to the Coroner's Office to retrieve the cornet for the memorial service. He took a look at it to see how badly dented the bell might be." She beamed at Jack. "He assured me that it would look like new when Mr. Stein was finished with it. Dr. Harrison gave us the mouthpiece to put into the case, but when we looked at it, it was the wrong size. A Benjamin Bent Model mouthpiece had specifically been ordered. Amanda knew this to be the size mouthpiece that Miss Blackthorne played from their private lessons."

"And that is what Mr. Stein and I put into the case. Though I was right there when Mrs. Tudor was wrapping the case, I was distracted for a moment by one of the draymen asking where he should put a delivery of newly arrived soprano saxophones. Mrs. Tudor must have had the substitute mouthpiece in her shop smock pocket and made the switch then," shared Mr. Ritberger.

Jack spoke up. "We think that the substitute mouthpiece was originally Mrs. Tudor's. Mr. O'Toole remembers the two sisters coming into the store with their father. He played a Model 19 Conn mouthpiece. Daniel keeps records on all of these things."

Looking at the gathered group Vashti concluded, "It truly was the last rose of summer."

# Vashti's Vittles

The city of Philadelphia had an important harbor where merchant ships brought unique goods from around the world. This gave people in the city a wider variety of foods, like other large cities that had similar ports.

While exotic goods were available, Vashti's family would have purchased most of their daily needs from stores within a four or five block area. During the growing season, the produce in these stores was grown on local farms located just outside of the city. They were eating local.

In the kitchens of America, Domestic Science was practiced. Dorothea Dix, a nurse during the American Civil War, revolutionized patient care by advocating healthy meals for wounded soldiers. This laid the groundwork for what we now call nutrition.

The social aspect of group activities for women is highlighted in the meals throughout the book. These food experiences are laid out in a menu format, as this is how they are presented in The Last Rose of Summer. You certainly can purchase a number of the menu items, rather than making them from scratch, but it's half the fun knowing how families and friends gathered around food, fun and music. So, gather your band members together and try all of the recipes that follow. Experience a little slice of how life may have tasted about a one hundred and twenty years ago, and be sure to tune in some lively marches as you dine.

## Picnic Meal

In the late 1800's drive-through meals didn't exist, so packing a lunch was the norm. Families that had more income could have bought food at the parks where they went to enjoy their weekend time off, but many immigrant families were counting pennies to try to buy a house or send a child to college.

## Sarsaparilla and Root Beer

A glass of sarsaparilla & root beer would have been very special. These were not everyday drinks. Milk for children and tea or coffee for adults were the most common drinks in households around 1900. A picnic where one could enjoy these special drinks would have been a tremendous treat.

## Knackwurst

Knack is the German word for "snap". In Vashti's lifetime this sausage would have been 100% pork. Today you can find it in various combinations of pork, veal and beef. It is usually made from better cuts of meat. Marjorum was a predominant spice along with salt, pepper and dried mustard. The "snap" is developed when the meat is put into natural casings and then boiled. The skin becomes taught and snaps when you bite it. It is often fully cooked and may be served room temperature, or hot, often grilled.

## Frankfurters

This is sometimes known as Vienna sausage, or Rindswurst. It is essentially a fully cooked sausage that looks a bit like an American hotdog. In Germany it is made of 100 percent pork and, by German law, true frankfurters must be produced within the city of Frankfurt or its surrounding area. In the United States it will be different, but no less tasty. Mustard is the most common condiment served with frankfurters.

### Dusseldorf Mustard

¼ cup yellow mustard seed
2 tablespoons brown mustard seeds (heaping)
¼ cup dry mustard
½ cup water
1½ cups cider vinegar
1 small onion chopped
2 tablespoons firmly packed brown sugar
1 teaspoon salt

2 garlic cloves minced
½ teaspoon ground cinnamon
¼ teaspoon ground allspice
¼ teaspoon dried tarragon leaves
⅛ teaspoon turmeric

1) In a glass bowl combine the mustard seeds and the dry mustard.

2) Using a non-aluminum pan combine all of the remaining ingredients. Simmer on medium heat until reduced by half.

3) Pour the hot liquid over the mustard mixture.

4) Cover loosely and let stand at room temperature for 24 to 48 hours. Keep the seeds covered with the mixture. You may need to add a little more vinegar.

5) Scrape the mixture into a blender and process for about 3 minutes. Blend longer for a smoother texture. You may need to add more vinegar. It will thicken as it stands.

6) Pour the mustard into clean, dry jars and allow to age, at room temperature, again. This aging period should be at least three days. The longer it ages, the mellower it becomes. Taste it every couple of days. When it reaches the level of spiciness that you like, refrigerate it. Putting it in the refrigerator stops the aging process.

## German Potato Salad

One of the important facets of the ladies' band was the mix of European ethnic groups. The social aspect of the band brought together young women of different social status. Their homes were decorated differently and their foods were of a great variety as well.

3 pounds red salad potatoes (1 to 2 inches across)
1 tablespoon of salt (for the potato water)
4 or 5 bacon slices
1 large white onion, diced
½ cup sugar
½ cup white vinegar (scant)

½ cup water (scant)
1 tablespoon salt (for the sauce)
1 teaspoon freshly cracked black pepper
½ cup of finely diced celery (optional)
2 tablespoons unsalted butter

Potatoes:
1) Wash the potatoes, but do not peel them. Cut the potatoes in uniform, bite-sized piece so they will cook evenly. Place them in a pot with just enough water to cover. Add a tablespoon of salt to the pot. Bring the pot of potatoes to a boil. Test after 8 minutes by poking with a fork. It should enter easily. If not done at 8 minutes, test every minute, or so, until they pass the fork test. Drain. Place in a large mixing bowl, set aside and cover with a dish towel to keep warm.

Slurry:
½ cup hot water
2 tablespoons flour

2) While the potatoes are cooking, place the flour in a bowl. Add the hot water and whisk until completely combined. Set aside.

3) Cut 4 or 5 slices of bacon into 1 inch pieces. In a medium sized pan, fry until golden brown, but not too dark. Drain off any excess bacon grease.

4) Finely dice 1 large white onion. Add it to the bacon and cook until it is lightly transparent.

5) Add sugar, vinegar, water, salt and freshly cracked black pepper. Bring to a boil.

6) A little at a time stir the slurry into the hot bacon sauce. Stir periodically until you get the desired thickness. About 5 minutes.

7) Here you may add celery to the bacon mixture if desired.

8) Stir the butter into the hot bacon sauce to create a glossy texture.

9) Mix with the warm potatoes. Using a slotted spoon, transfer to a serving bowl. If there is excess discard it. Serve warm.

## Sauerkraut

1 medium head of green cabbage
¼ cup kosher salt
bottled water
1 tablespoon caraway seeds (optional)

1) Wash the cabbage and take off any leaves that are wilted.

2) Cut the cabbage in half and remove the hard core.

3) Slice the cabbage into thin strips.

4) Place the cabbage in a glass bowl and add the salt. Using your hands, rub the salt into the cabbage. It will wilt down and start to exude juice.

5) Pack the cabbage into a sterilized quart, canning jar. Add the juice from the bowl. If the juice does not cover the cabbage, add a little more water. Note: Do not use tap water that has been softened. Use bottled water instead.

6) Put in a dark place and allow this to ferment. Test it to see if you like the sharpness that has developed every three days. It becomes more sour the longer it ferments. When it has reached your desired taste, you may add the caraway seeds.

7) Cover with a sterilized lid and process in a water bath.

## Picnic Sandwiches

Sandwiches are the original fast food. You made them ahead and were able to grab and go for your lunch. The pickle functions as a palate cleanser.

## Liver Sausage Sandwich

4 slices white sandwich bread
3 ounces liver sausage
3 hard-boiled eggs
1 dill pickle spear
Chives to garnish (optional)

1) Put the liver sausage, hard-boiled eggs and pickle in a food processor and blend until smooth.

2) Lay out 4 slices of bread.

3) Spread a thin layer of the spread onto the bread. If using the chives cut them into tiny pieces. Sprinkle a few on each sandwich.

4) Cut each slice diagonally to create little triangles for a nice presentation.

## Swiss Cheese Sandwich

8 slices marble rye bread
Swiss cheese, sliced thinly
Leafy lettuce, washed
3 tablespoons mayonnaise
2 teaspoons mustard
Dill pickles for garnish

1) In a small bowl, mix together the mayonnaise and mustard.

2) Lay out 4 slices of bread. Cover the slice with lettuce.

3) Smooth some of the mayonnaise and mustard mixture on the lettuce. This keeps the bread from getting soggy.

4) Put a layer of Swiss cheese over the mustard and out to the edges of the bread.

5) Cover the cheese with the remaining bread slices.

6) One dill pickle is set on the plate with each sandwich.

## Budget Breakfast

## German Raw Fried Potatoes

6 small, new potatoes (do not peel)
3 tablespoons of bacon fat
1 teaspoon salt
¼ teaspoon pepper
Green onions or chives for garnish (optional)

1) Wash the potatoes, and slice them very thinly. Cover with cold water and allow to sit for 20 minutes. Drain and dry the potatoes.

2) Melt the bacon fat over medium heat in a cast iron skillet. When the fat is melted, add the potatoes and seasonings. Cover tightly, lower the heat and allow to steam for 20 to 25 minutes, stirring once.

3) When brown at the bottom, turn and brown the other side.

Chopped green onion or chive may be added for garnish.

## Bacon ends

Today we buy bacon from peek-a-boo window packages so you can see the meat to fat ratio. Back in Vashti's day you would go to your local butcher to purchase the amount of bacon that you needed. He would cut a chunk off for you. He might slice it too. The end of the bacon chunk was not as easy to put into the slicer and it would be sold for less money. The smart shopper bought the bacon end because it was less expensive, but just as tasty.

## Bacon gravy

To extend a meal, gravy was often added. This is an easy use for the bacon fat. It isn't low calorie, but that wasn't as much of a concern in the 1890's.

The amount of flour you use will depend on the amount of bacon fat that is rendered.
Start with 2 tablespoons of flour.

1) In the skillet, where the bacon was cooked, add a tablespoon of flour.

2) Whisk the flour into the bacon fat until it forms gravy.

3) Add an additional tablespoon of flour until it develops the consistency that you like. The amount you add will depend on how much fat was rendered from the bacon.

Pour over the potatoes or serve on the side.

### Fortifying Breakfast

Eggs were readily available, especially in the spring and summer. When it gets cold, really cold, the hens cease to lay eggs. This is a meal for the times of year when eggs were plentiful. Did those people one hundred, or so, years ago know about protein? Cholesterol?

## Fried Eggs

2 large eggs
2 tablespoons butter
Salt and pepper to taste

1) Melt the butter in a frying pan over medium low heat.

2) Crack the eggs into a small bowl, being careful not to get any shell in with the eggs.

There are many ways to cook eggs. Here are the two styles requested by the O'Brien men.

3A) **Sunny side up:** When the butter is melted, carefully slide the eggs into the pan without breaking the yolks. As the butter gets hotter you will see the whites start to turn white. When the white is set remove them with a spatula. You can serve them on top of the toast to catch the yolk, or use the toast to dab it up.

3B) **Over easy:** Follow steps 1 and 2 above. Then, carefully slide the eggs into the pan, being careful not to break the yolks. As the white starts to set and the yolk develops a little film, carefully flip the eggs over using a spatula. Cook for one more minute.

## Toast

Mrs. O'Brien makes toast on the cast iron stove. In the old days there were little built-in racks on the stove for making toast. They were in the back by the chimney. You had to watch it closely or it would burn and you had to flip it over to toast the second side. Today we'd just use a toaster. Hearty bread such as Irish soda bread could have been the norm. Not the easily squished white bread that so many of us grew up on.

## Irish Soda Bread

3¼ cups all-purpose flour
4 tablespoons granulated sugar
1 teaspoon baking soda
1 teaspoon baking powder
½ teaspoon salt
½ cup butter (1 stick), softened
1 cup buttermilk
1 egg
⅛ cup unsalted butter, melted
⅛ cup buttermilk

1) Preheat your oven to 350°.

2) Lightly grease a large baking sheet pan.

3) In a large bowl, mix the flour, sugar, baking soda, baking powder, salt.

4) Mix in softened butter.

5) Add 1 cup of buttermilk and the egg, mixing until it forms a soft dough.

6) Turn out onto a lightly floured surface and knead gently.

7) Form the dough into a disk and flattened to about ½ inch thick.

8) Place on the prepared baking pan.

9) In a small bowl combine the melted butter with the ¼ cup of buttermilk. Brush this mixture on the top of the loaf.

10) Using a sharp knife, cut an X into the top of the loaf.

11) Place in the oven. At 30 minutes check for doneness by inserting a toothpick into the center. If it does not come out clean, continue baking, checking at about 5 minute intervals. If it does come out clean, remove from oven and cool on a rack, or enjoy it hot.

## Bacon

Bacon was a staple in most diets. It was easily preserved as it was smoked or could be cured with salt. You could hang it in the pantry and it would keep for quite some time.

To fry bacon:

1) Allow bacon to sit at room temperature for five minutes before frying.

2) Using a cold frying pan, lay the strips of bacon in single layers so they don't touch.

3) Turn the heat on to low. You will notice that the fat begins to exude from the bacon strips.

4) When the bacon edges start to curl, flip the strips over.

5) Continue to cook until it reaches the level of doneness that you like.

6) Remove to a paper towel to drain. Serve hot.

## Luncheon

Nothing ever went to waste in kitchens. Great care was given to using everything and to exercising economy in the kitchen. Fortunately for the food lover, the ham bone was often used for soup. If you had a ham for a Sunday meal, the bone was saved for soup. Today's cook uses a ham shank for soup.

### Split pea soup

1 or 2 ham shanks weighing 2 pounds
1 medium carrot, washed and diced
1 medium white onion, peeled and quartered
2 whole potatoes, peeled (russets work well)
3 quarts boiling water (or home made chicken stock)
4 large sprigs of parsley
1 clove garlic
1 bay leaf
½ teaspoon fresh thyme (or ¼ dried thyme)
2 cups split peas (soaked overnight)
½ teaspoon salt
½ teaspoon white pepper

1) Spread the peas out on a cookie sheet and check for stones. Discard any you may find. Place split peas in a large bowl and cover with cold water. Soak overnight.

2) In a large stockpot place the ham bone, carrot, onion, potatoes, bay leaf, garlic clove, parsley and thyme. Cover with the boiling water (or stock). Boil for one hour, skimming off foam, if necessary.

3) Strain and reserve the stock.

4) Rinse the ham bone in hot water. Cut any remaining meat off the bone and into bite-sized pieces. Return the meat to the ham stock, discard the bone.

5) Drain the split peas and add them to the stock. Boil for one hour. If the split peas have not melted down, use a submersible blender to puree them.

6) Season with salt and pepper. Taste and adjust the seasoning to your liking.

## Open-faced Watercress & Cream Cheese Sandwiches

½ cup watercress, plus a bit more for garnish
¼ cup butter, softened
4 ounces of cream cheese, softened
1 teaspoon fresh squeezed lemon juice
Pinch of freshly cracked black pepper
White bread

1) In a food processor finely chop ½ cup of watercress. Add lemon juice, butter, cream cheese and pepper. Blend until smooth, scrape down the sides of the bowl and give it one last spin*.

2) Allow the mixture to stand at room temperature for half and hour to develop it's flavor.

3) Slice the white bread thinly. Remove the crusts.

4) Spread a thin layer of the cheese mixture on the bread. Cut each slide into quarters and garnish with a sprig of watercress.

*At this point you may refrigerate the spread for a day. Allow the spread to come to room temperature before assembling the sandwiches.

## Boiled cabbage

4 cups water
1 small cabbage cut into 8 pieces. Leave the core in to hold the leaves together.
1 white onion, diced
2 tablespoon of butter
1 teaspoon salt
Pinch of pepper
2 tablespoons flour

1) In a three-quart saucepan heat 4 cups of water to boiling.

2) Melt butter in a large casserole over medium high heat.

3) Add onion to the casserole and caramelize.

4) Add cabbage and about ½ cup of boiling water to the onion, cover and steam for about 10 minutes.

5) After 10 minutes pour enough boiling water over the cabbage to cover.

6) Add salt and pepper and boil until tender. The tip of a knife should enter the cabbage easily.

7) Sprinkle with flour, stir and boil a little longer to create a sauce.

Serve hot.

## Roast Beef Sandwiches with pickles

Did you ever wonder why there is a pickle on the plate of many sandwiches? The tartness of the pickle is meant to cut the richness of meats and/or cheese. It was also thought to aid in digestion. Jack O'Brien chooses a roast beef sandwich at the Horn & Hardart. You can make your life a little easier by buying thinly sliced meat from your butcher. Thin is an important element to the sandwich. Should you choose to roast your own beef, be sure to slice it thinly.

1 loaf, white crusty bread
1 pound of thinly sliced roast beef
Butter (the best you can find), softened
Dill pickles to garnish

1) Cut the bread into ½ inch slices.

2) Butter the bread out to the edges.

3) Loosely pile 2 or 3 slices of beef on the bread. Fold them over loosely. You want the air in between slices.

4) Place the top piece of bread, butter side down, on the first slice. If the bread slices are large, you may want to cut the sandwich in half. Put it on a plate and add a crisp dill pickle to garnish.

## Dinner or Supper

Depending on where you live, the last meal of the day may have a different name. Did you grow up with the phrase breakfast, lunch and supper? How about breakfast, lunch and dinner? In Vashi's world it was very likely breakfast, dinner and supper. Tea would have been served around 4 pm and supper at 7 or 8 pm.

## Consome'

The traditional recipe for consome' takes hours and hours to make. Here is a short cut for the 21st century home cook.

1 can of good quality beef broth
2 tablespoons of Port wine

1) In a heavy saucepan, bring the broth and the wine just to a boil.

2) Serve hot in a large soup bowl.

## Olives & celery

These are easy sides to the meal. The celery would have been served cold like we would see on a relish tray today. The olives could have been of any variety. Many were available. The sourness of the olives in pickling brine paired well with the roasted pig.

## Cold roast pig

Domestic Science taught the principle of planning meals for the week. It also taught the use of meats in second meals.

Pork roast comes in several shapes and sizes including loin, shoulder, leg and, the all-important ham. This meal features cold meat, and the ham would work very well as it slices beautifully.

3 pounds cooked ham

1) Carve the ham very thinly and arrange it beautifully on a platter to pass at the table.

## Vienna Rolls

If you cannot find a Vienna roll, buy Kaiser rolls. This is a hard roll that is similar to a Vienna roll. Use the following to create a Vienna roll.

1 dozen Kaiser rolls
1 tablespoon cornstarch
3 tablespoons water
2 teaspoon caraway seed
3 teaspoons course salt

1) Preheat oven to 375 degrees.

2) Mix the cornstarch and water together in a small bowl.

3) Brush each roll on top with the cornstarch mixture.

4) Sprinkle with coarse salt and caraway seed.

5) Bake for 2 minutes.

## Escaloped Oysters

1 pint fresh oysters
1 cup heavy cream, divided
½ cup dry breadcrumbs
1 cup cracker crumbs
½ cup butter, melted
¼ teaspoon Worcestershire sauce
¼ teaspoon salt
Pinch of fresh cracked black pepper

1) Preheat oven to 350 degrees.

2) Butter a shallow backing dish.  A gratin dish works well.

3) Mix bread and cracker crumbs.

4) Stir the butter into the cracker mixture until all the crumbs are moist.

5) Put a third of the crumb mixture in the prepared baking dish pressing down lightly.

6) Cover the crumb with half of the oysters and sprinkle with salt and pepper.

7) In a large bowl, mix the heavy cream and Worcestershire sauce together.  Pour half of it over the oysters in the baking pan.

8) Repeat steps five through seven.

9) Cover with remaining crumbs.

10) Bake for 30 to 40 minutes.

## Brick Cheese

This is an old school cheese that was definitely available in Philadelphia. If you can't find brick cheese, try to find a very young Muenster cheese. Slice it thinly.

## Candied Walnuts

1 cup whole walnuts
2 tablespoons butter
2 tablespoons sugar
½ teaspoon sea salt
¼ teaspoon cinnamon (optional)

1) In a heavy bottom pan heat to medium high heat and melt the butter.

2) Add walnuts and mix until they are covered with butter.

3) Sprinkle in the sugar and cinnamon, if using.

4) Continue to stir until caramelized, about 3 or 4 minutes.

5) Pour out onto parchment paper. Sprinkle with sea salt. Separate and cool.

6) Store in an airtight container.

# Tea Service

Tea was served at 4 or 5 pm. It was a little pick-me-up that tided one over until supper. It could be very simple tea and some light cookies or a more substantial repast as in The Last Rose of Summer.

Vashti and her mother shop for the petits fours, but they could have made them as well. They are not hard to do, but a little time consuming. They can be made ahead and kept for several days.

## Petits fours

The name of these delectable treats means "small oven." This harkens back to 17th century France when the only people who had ovens were the village bakers. These ovens were large, stone structures that had no temperature controls. Different baked goods were put into the oven based on the temperature they required. When the oven was fired up it could reach 800 to 1000 degrees Fahrenheit. The embers were allowed to cool a bit before the breads went in during the middle time. As the embers died down even more, the oven was considered to be "small". That is when these delectable cakes were baked.

2 cups all-purpose flour, sifted
3 teaspoons baking powder
¼ teaspoon salt
½ cup shortening
½ teaspoon vanilla
1 cup sugar
½ cup milk
4 egg whites, stiffly beaten

1) Preheat oven to 375 degrees and grease two 9-inch cake pans.

2) Sift together the flour, baking powder and salt.

3) In a mixer, cream the shortening, vanilla and sugar until fluffy.

4) Alternate adding the sifted ingredients and milk to the mixer.

5) Fold in the stiffly beaten egg whites by hand.

6) Pour batter into the pans.

7) Bake for 25 minutes, cool.

8) Cut into 2-inch squares.

9) Place wire racks over waxed paper. Arrange the squares about an inch apart on the racks.

## Frosting

1 egg white
1 teaspoon cold water
1 teaspoon vanilla
2 cups confectioner's sugar
green and red food coloring

1) In a medium sized bowl stir until blended the egg white, cold water and vanilla.

2) Gradually beat in 2 cups of confectioners sugar.

3) Divide into 2 pieces.

4) In separate bowls add green food coloring to one portion and red to the other. Mix until the color goes through the entire frosting. Option: Allow a portion of the frosting to remain white

5) Frost one of the cake rounds. Set the other round on top of it. Gently press down to assure that they stay together.

6) Cut the cakes into squares, rectangles, triangles or any interesting shapes. They should be bitesize.

7) Frost each piece and decorate with a piece of dried fruit or nutmeat, etc.

## Optional toppings

Nutmeats
Candied fruit
Coconut
Small pieces of candy

## Sweets

## Salt-water Taffy

Salt-water taffy doesn't contain any salt. An urban legend tells of a candy storeowner on the New Jersey shore who had his entire store soaked during an 1883 storm. He joked about having "salt-water" taffy and the name stuck.

Unless you are looking for an upper body workout, find a good confectioner for your salt-water taffy. There are many fun flavors.

**Ice Cream Sundae**

Our mystery took place in July. Raspberries could have been one of the fruits available to top the sundaes, but they likely also had other toppings:

Chopped pecans
Hershey's chocolate syrup (It's Pennsylvania, after all)
Strawberry sauce
Crushed pineapple
Caramel

Vanilla ice cream was the flavor of choice, but you could provide other tastes for your guests. Try creating an ice cream sundae station for your guests.

1) Put out parfait dishes, ice cream scoopers and spoons.

2) Set the ice cream out about 10 minutes before serving so it will soften.

3) Have a tall container filled with warm water where your guests may dip the scoopers before digging into the ice cream. It helps the ice cream to release more easily from the scooper.

4) Display the toppings in pretty bowls with double stations of each, or 2 spoons to speed up the process.

5) Alternately, you may designate an “official scooper” to help the flow of traffic and keep the party moving along.

Patricia Backhaus may be found on Facebook
Cornetpat@aol.com

Made in the USA
Middletown, DE
05 April 2018